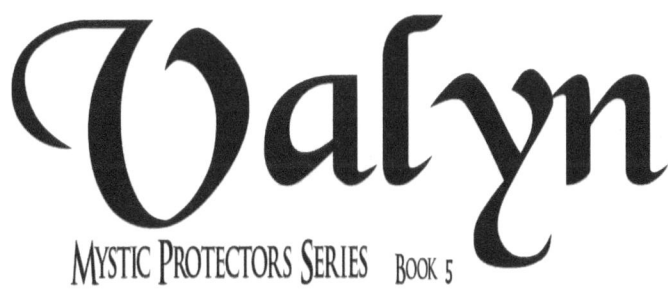

Valyn

MYSTIC PROTECTORS SERIES BOOK 5

KATHI S. BARTON

World Castle Publishing, LLC
Pensacola, Florida
Copyright © Kathi S. Barton 2018
Paperback ISBN: 9781629899435
eBook ISBN: 9781629899442
First Edition World Castle Publishing, LLC, June 25, 2018
http://www.worldcastlepublishing.com
Licensing Notes
Cover: Karen Fuller
Editor: Maxine Bringenberg

CHAPTER 1

Jenny didn't open her mouth except to put food in it. Drinking water was done through a straw, and she didn't count that as opening her mouth. The woman in the room with her, another cop, asked her if she wanted anything. Jenny didn't bother answering her.

She'd been in the hospital for five days now, in a private room with a television and a nice couch, and chair. They were much nicer and in better shape than the ones she had in her apartment. But here she was chained to the bed, and not able to go home and be on her own not so comfy furniture.

The winged man asked her how she was feeling. He'd not left her side once since she'd been brought here. And the fact that no one else could see him gave her the willies. She didn't talk to him either, but he sure did talk to her. And most of it was about the day in the diner.

"The man you killed—rightfully—would have killed all those people in that diner if not for you." She huffed

5

at him. "He would have, and you saved them. Whatever they're holding you for, it's going to be finished very soon. I promise you."

Jenny glared at him and he smiled. She had no idea why she found him to be charming. Most of the time she didn't go for that. But this man, for some reason, made her feel safe and secure. It was really too bad that he wasn't real.

She remembered every detail about the day that things had gone to shit. Every second seemed to be burned into her mind — even the face, the half face of the man that she'd killed by shooting him with his own gun. She didn't think that would be anything that she'd ever forget. But, it was kill him or be killed.

All she wanted to do was make enough money that she could have a good meal. Not even to go out to dinner and such, but to be able to afford enough groceries so she could eat better. To say that she wasn't making ends meet would be a gross understatement. She barely had a roof over her head when the rent came due.

Rolling to her side as best she could with her leg wrapped up and the handcuff on her leg, Jenny thought about what it would be like not to have to worry about every little thing that came along. Like a coat for winter that didn't need to have furnace tape on it to cover the holes. Or boots that were just a little too snug and put blisters on her toes. Being hauled into court over this credit card, one that she'd never seen or used, had taken all she had, and a great deal that she didn't. Perhaps, she thought, she should have let the man kill her.

"Don't think like that." She looked at the man in front of her. His wings were impressive, and she wanted to touch them to see if they were real. "You mustn't think like that. You are going to be so much better than you are now."

Closing her eyes against the pain that his words brought her, Jenny felt the tears roll down her cheeks. Nothing was ever going to be better, and she knew it as surely as she was lying there. When the door opened, she didn't even bother looking up.

"Miss Hale." She looked at the cop, Benny Anderson, the one that had locked her to this bed. "I've come to apologize to you and to take the cuffs off. We shouldn't have ever put them on you."

"Is this a trick?" He shook his head and smiled. "If it's all the same to you, I'd rather you didn't talk to me. You've been hounding me for days now, and I don't particularly like you."

"Really? My wife says that I'm charming, when I want to be." She only huffed at him and the female officer left them. "Yes, well, you're right on that one when I locked you up. But I did have a reason for doing it. You would have left here the first day you were admitted, wouldn't you have?"

"I can't afford this. And I'm pretty sure that you know it." Benny nodded and glanced to her left at the winged man. "Is he real?"

Benny looked at her with the strangest smile. But he only nodded. A million and one questions came to her in that second, but she wasn't sure that she trusted herself or this man enough to ask them. Instead, she looked at the winged man.

"His name is Arryn. He's a protector." Jenny tore her eyes away from Arryn and looked at Benny again. "He's here to watch over you while you're here. And there are more like him to take care of you when you leave."

Closing her eyes again, she thought of someone watching over her. It would have been a lot easier had someone been watching her since she left home ten years ago. Benny was talking to Arryn, and she tried to calm her mind down enough to think. It was difficult when all she could think about was how much this stay in the hospital was going to cost her.

Arryn sat in the chair that was in her line of sight. "I'd like to talk to you about some things. Is that all right? Benny has gone now, but he'll be back later with his wife. You'll like her, she's one of us." She asked him just what that was. "I used to be a Protector, someone that watched over an assigned person or animal from birth until they passed onto the next part of their journey. But now, I'm call a Mystic. I'm training new Protectors on how to manage in the real world, your world, so they can figure out how to blend in when they're here."

"I think I would have noticed winged people all around." He told her that she wasn't meant to see them. "I see. Actually, no I don't. You want to help them blend in, but no one sees them. What does that even mean?"

"We sometimes take a break. We take them when our charge, the one we've been chosen to watch over, passes from this life to the next level. It's hard, spending a great many years with someone and not get to know and love them. So the break is necessary so that we can get back in the rotations and go with another being." She asked him why she could see him. "You're not dead, if that's what you're thinking. I could look, but I won't do that again unless you stop talking to me. You can see me because of your future. You're going to be the mate to one of my kind. Do you understand what a mate is?"

"You mean a slave to someone. Thanks, but no thanks. My mother was a slave to my father, and I'm never going to go through that. Never." Arryn told her that it wasn't like that. "Sure it's not. And this other man, this other Protector, he's going to take care of me? I bet that this job you say you have, it more than likely doesn't pay much, does it? And that I'm going to have to find a job to support us both. As I said before, thanks but no thanks."

"It pays very well." She didn't bother asking him what sort of *well* he thought it was. "You're very hard to reason with. Has anyone told you that before?"

"No. I'm not usually so untrusting. But you being a winged man while I'm in a hospital room that I can ill afford while I wonder where I'm going to work, or even if I have a place to go back to, that makes me a little hostile." He laughed. It was a beautiful sound, one that she thought she could hear a great deal and never tire of it. "Why don't you go bother someone else? As soon as I'm out of here, I have a shit load of stuff to do. And being here, it's not going to pay my rent or feed me. I don't usually have enough to do the latter of that, but I need to find a job."

The door opened, and a beautiful woman came in. She glowed, like a million lights were shining on her. And when she smiled, it was breathtaking. Jenny was afraid to acknowledge her. What if she was as unreal as the rest of this?

"Hello, Jenny. My name is Lily. I'm the wife of Benny Anderson. The detective that brought you here." Jenny shook her hand and felt something profound run over her body. It wasn't painful, but it was certainly a lot of something. "Oh, you're going to be so good for Valyn. He's expecting you, but doesn't know where you are or when you're coming."

"Is that the man that expects me to wait on him hand and foot? If it is, I'd rather he didn't know where I was at all." Lily just smiled. It was becoming irritating the way they thought a smile was the cure all to everything. "I think you both should leave me alone now. I'm hoping to get myself out of here soon. As much as you probably expect me to say it's been fun, it hasn't. You two are bonkers."

This time she heard different laughter. Looking around for the source, she knew that she'd gone off the deep end. But the man sitting in the chair, one that hadn't been there before, was still laughing. He asked the other two to leave them alone, that he'd keep an eye on her for a little while.

"You're very lucky. And smart." Jenny didn't know what to say to him, so she kept her mouth shut. "I wanted to tell you about Valyn. He's my—I guess you could call him my next project."

"If it's all the same to you, I don't want to be someone's lab rat in a project." He laughed again, and for some odd reason, Jenny thought that he didn't do that very much. "Who are you?"

"They all call me Boss. I have come to like the term. It so much friendlier than anything else I might go by. I've really come to calm your mind about a great many things. If you would allow me to, that is." She nodded, not even sure that she could have told him no. "There's a good girl. Valyn, he's one of the most generous and kind men I have had the pleasure of working with. I think that you and he will get along famously. But he's been heavy in his heart for some time now. I think you're the one to pull him from it all."

"I don't want to pull anyone out of anything. In the event you might not know, I don't have a pot to piss in, and not enough money to even begin to pay this bill." He snapped his fingers and handed her the paper that suddenly appeared. It said that her stay here was paid in full. "What did you do? Screw around on a computer to do this? I won't be a part of anything illegal. You fix it."

"The bill has been paid. There is no screwing around on anyone's part. I paid it. And I'd do it again for you if you needed it." She still didn't trust him. "I'd like for you to listen to me for a bit. I would like to tell you what you're coming into with Valyn."

"I see. You've paid off my bill so that I'd have no choice other than to go to this man and be his slave." He asked her why she thought she'd be a slave. "I know what I am, Mr. Boss. A nobody that has nothing. And men that would want a nobody like me are usually either drunks, thieves, or a combination of both. I don't need the extra pressure put on me. I don't have it in me."

"You're much stronger than you give yourself credit

for. Why, you saved a great many people when you killed Edward. You have no idea how grateful I am to you." She said it was only a few people. "No. What you don't know, and very few would, is that he wasn't going to be killed by the police as he so wanted. But he was going to leave the diner after killing everyone, including you, and murder thirty-one more people before he killed himself. You also saved three police officers that tried to take him in, as well as two people that would have been so injured by his bullets that they would never able to walk again."

"You mean, he could have done those things. There isn't any way that you'd know that for sure." He only nodded, and Jenny believed him. Looking around the room, she spoke to him again. "Why is this happening to me? I feel like I'm on some kind of rollercoaster that never ends."

"A very long time ago you saved a small child. Do you remember that?" Nodding, Jenny looked at him. "She had no more idea than you did at the time what she was going to come to mean to a great many people. Her knowledge and will to get to the bottom of things has made her into a great woman. She has saved so many lives because of what she does. And that is all thanks to you. You could have let her lay there and die, but you carried the small bundle to the hospital and left her there to get care. When you yourself needed much more than she did at the time. Your parents had taken a whip to you for not making a good grade on a spelling test."

"It was the one and only time that I showed them my work from school. I got all A's all the time. And the spelling test had an A- on it. That pissed them off and they hurt me. Again." Mr. Boss nodded, the look on his face full of sadness. "I was determined to run away. To hide from them until I turned eighteen. At nine years old that seemed like a lifetime away. But I saw her in the trashcan and took her there. I knew that she'd be helped."

"And she did get it." Mr. Boss grinned at her. "You need to stop calling me Mr. Boss. Even in your head. I'm just Boss."

Jenny laid her head back on the pillow. Watching the man as he sat there, she grew sleepier and sleepier. When he told her to let go, to rest and he'd be back, Jenny let the exhaustion that she'd been feeling since she was brought here take her under.

Valyn was just putting up the last piece of drywall when he felt someone in the room with him. Janie Preston had been coming up all the stairs twice an hour to ask him a question about this or that. He knew that she was nervous, working at a different job than she'd had before, but he wanted her to just yell for him rather than go up and down the stairs.

"You can call the store for them to deliver anything that you want. Or do the click and pay thing that Renie set up for you. It's okay if you overorder, we'll fix it." When she didn't answer him, he turned to look. Boss was leaning against the door jam and smiling. "You can go away too. This is my down time and I'm using it wisely. Unless you came here to grant my request."

"Nay, I have not. And I told you already that I will

not put you to sleep for an eternity. You're doing a fine job with this. I remember once before you were a carpenter." Valyn went back to work. "I've talked to your mate."

That got his attention. But instead of asking Boss anything about her, he continued working. Of course, he thought that was just as funny. Finally, having finished with the sheet, Valyn set his trowel down and looked at him. The man was in an entirely too good of a mood for him to deal with right now.

"I've told you, several times already, that I have no wish for a mate. I'm broken." He'd only say that to Boss, and it pained Valyn when he did. "You'll have to tell her that you've made a mistake."

Cocking his brow at him, Boss just stared. Valyn, usually not one to squirm when being examined as he was now, wanted to lock himself in a room until Boss left. But he knew that he'd not leave until he said or did what he'd come for.

"She's a lovely girl. Broken too, if you want to know the truth of it. Perhaps you've heard her mentioned. She's the woman that saved that diner full of patrons about a week ago." He'd heard of it but didn't know her name. "The bill collectors are hounding her hourly. However, they are not putting the calls through to her room at the hospital for fear of upsetting her. She's made some very good friends while staying there."

"What happened to her?" He told him what she'd done and how she'd been shot. "And the bill collectors? Why are they hounding her? I'm assuming that she has debt, but it's more than that, isn't it?"

"Yes. She's now homeless and jobless. Also, with this other business of the credit card, there is no way that she can make anything work out right for her. Not without a great deal of help." Valyn sat down on the wire wheel that had been left behind when the house had been rewired. "Valyn, you told me that you were broken and why you thought so. But this woman, she can help you in ways that I cannot."

"You could if you would just put me to sleep." Boss shook his head. "What if I don't go and see her? Don't take her as my mate? Because I don't think my life could be any better to have her with me. I'm not good around people anymore. I don't want to have someone depending on me for their wellbeing. It's too much."

"Nay, it is not. And you are very strong, just tired." Valyn found that he wanted to cry. It had been too long ago that he'd even thought about having something for himself. "Go and see her. You don't have to show yourself. But see that what I tell you is the truth."

"I can't." Boss nodded and said that he understood. Then he was gone. "I don't need someone depending on me. Can't you see that?"

He was talking to air, he knew that, but he really didn't want to have to deal, or whatever needed to be done, with another person. He'd had about all that he could work with in his time here on Earth, and he didn't want to tackle having a mate too. Getting up, he stretched his back and walked to the second room that he'd been working on.

The walls in this room were all right. In fact, the ones that he'd been replacing in the other room were fine too.

But it was nice to be able to work with his body again. To lift and stretch muscles that had not been used in a few decades.

Going downstairs, he saw that Janie was making an order for the grocery store to deliver. He got himself a glass of tea after telling her that he had it. Janie asked him if he wanted something to eat, that she had a pot pie all ready for him to have.

"Yes, that would be great." She nodded and went to the oven as he sat down at the little table in this room. "I'm not having your meal, am I? I don't want to do that to you."

"No, I've eaten already. It's well after two, and I was just waiting for you to come down." He told her he was sorry. "Don't be. You are a smart man and would have, sooner or later, come here to eat. I was ready for you."

They talked about what he liked and didn't like, which wasn't all that much in the dislike column. He did tell her that he enjoyed salads a great deal, and that he'd like to have them on occasion. She beamed with happiness to have him give her something to make for him. Valyn worried about a great many things lately, and very little of it did he have any control over.

"I've got myself a mate." He had told her when he'd rescued her from the bank one afternoon what he was, and begged her to keep his secret. "She's in the hospital after being shot by a would-be madman."

"The Hale woman?" He didn't know her name and told her so. "Jennifer Hale is her name if it's the same woman. She was shot by the man before she ended up killing him with his own gun. I heard that she's recuperating, and should be released from the hospital soon."

"I don't want her." Janie didn't say anything, but he could feel her confusion. "I'm not a well man. I've seen too much and done much more. I can't have someone in my life that could be hurt by my unwillingness to be something that I'm not."

"And what is it you think she'd want from you, Valyn? She has nothing, from what I've heard. And she's out of work, as the owner of the place that she worked has closed the restaurant down as of the day that Mr. Goodman came in." He told her what Boss had told him. "Oh, so you think that she'll want all your money. From what I've been made to understand, you have more than you could spend in several lifetimes. Not that it makes it right if that is what she wants, but I highly doubt that. And I'm sure you don't believe it either."

"I wouldn't think so." He ate a few bites of the pot pie before shoving it away. Janie pushed it right back at him and told him to eat. "I'm not a child that needs to have a mother figure making me eat."

"Then perhaps you should stop acting like one and get your ass in gear." He was shocked by her words, and when she stood up and went to the computer, he had the overwhelming urge to cry again. "You have someone out there that could make every hurt that you have seem like nothing. A person that, from what I've seen, will love you despite your being a baby about things. And here you sit on your ass, whining about being broken. Well, how do you think she feels right now?"

"Why are you talking to me this way? You work for

me." She asked him if he wanted her to quit in order to talk to him like he deserved. "I don't deserve any of this. I didn't ask for her to come into my life."

"Then you're going to be as broken as you think you are now."

Leaving the kitchen, Valyn made his way out to the yard. It was cold this time of year, but he so loved the way the earth seemed to go to sleep and let the winter take control. He wanted to think, to clear his mind, but he had a feeling that he wouldn't. At least not until he saw this woman for himself. Instead of driving himself, which he was terrible at, he asked Renie to take him there, and she told him she'd be there in ten minutes.

Valyn hoped that he wasn't making the biggest mistake of his life by visiting this woman. But he knew as surely as he was standing there that she might just need him more than he needed her. And if it took all his money to make her secure in her life, then he'd gladly give it to her, so long as she didn't come into his life and expect more than he could give her. Love, he knew, was no longer an emotion that he had.

CHAPTER 2

She'd been released about an hour ago, and was still trying to figure out where she could go. Jenny was worried that the man, Mr. Boss, would come back to talk to her again. And the way she was feeling right now, she might go see this Valyn person. She had asked for and received the paperwork to get out of the hospital—against doctors' orders, of course.

After making a call from the hospital room that she'd been in, Jenny knew that she no longer had a place to go and all her things had been taken to hopefully sell off to make some of their money back. Jenny doubted that it would be enough to buy a paper, much less four hundred dollars in rent money.

The crutches were hurting her underarms, and she had to stop and rest every few steps because she was exhausted. And she hurt. There wasn't any money for any pain medication, and she still wasn't sure if the bill had actually been paid or not. Hobbling along, Jenny tried hard not to cry about all this crap going on in her life.

"Jennifer Hale?" She kept moving, sure this was going to be a person from the hospital demanding money for the bill. "Your bill has been taken care of. I thought that you'd been made aware of that."

Turning wasn't easy and she nearly fell and would have had the woman behind her not caught her. And when she had her standing again, the woman touched her fingers to her forehead and Jenny felt it all the way to the bottom of her feet. Staggering back, she was caught again, this time by a man she didn't know.

"My name is Kala Trainer, and this is my husband, Riss. I only needed to touch you to have a connection to you. We've come to bring you to our home." Kala looked at her like she thought it was a done deal, going to their home. But Jenny wasn't stupid, nor that desperate. "Yes, you are. And we both know that you don't have a home to go to, even to get warm."

"Stop reading my mind." She was pissed off now, and Jenny just wanted to be left alone. "I don't know you, and you just expect me to drop everything and go with you? No, I don't think so. I'll sleep in this alley before I do that."

Riss spoke from behind her. "Kala, do you think that she has any idea that there are terrible people hanging around here? Or does she have no care for herself? I hope that is not true."

"What do you want from me? Is this about that Valyn guy? If it is, I've already told that other man, Mr. Boss, that I don't want anything to do with any of you." She started to leave them there when the man picked her up in his arms.

The pain was incredible, and she only barely held onto her scream. "Are you nuts? You're not thinking of kidnapping me, are you? Because you may think I'm easy, but I'm not going to have any sick games with you."

"I do not wish to play with you at all." He looked at his wife and smiled. "I don't know what she means. Games are for children."

"She means that she won't have sex with you." The look on the man's face almost made it worth the pain she was in. Almost. Telling him that she was going to be sick made him set her down on her feet, and the pain of that fast movement had her screaming out in pain this time.

"Valyn, I don't think that is going to help her." The voices were quiet, but she could hear them easily enough. While she figured that she'd passed out, she didn't know where she was. "Don't do it."

"Do what?" Opening her eyes, she closed them again when the man standing over her looked so good. Too many men today seemed like they'd been carved from the strongest stone and looked good just for the hell of it. "Where am I?"

"You are in my home. In one of the bedrooms that I've only just finished working on." The strange voice had her thinking that this was the famous Valyn. Opening her eyes once more, she tried to sit up when she was pushed back on the softest bed she'd ever laid on. "You must lie still or you're going to open the wound again." She tried her best to struggle to sit up, only to be pushed back again.

"Listen here, buddy. I'm not a child, and I'd appreciate you not treating me like one. Get your hands off me." He

21

jerked his hand away immediately. Sitting up without anyone assisting her, Jenny felt pretty good about herself. But the pain was making itself known again. "Why am I here when I said, quite clearly, that I didn't want to come here? You do know that this is kidnapping, right?"

"You didn't want to go to Riss's home, so I brought you here. This isn't the place you were told about." She looked at him and wanted to punch him in the face. "You're very violent, aren't you? I was only trying to make a point that you were not kidnapped. I'm Valyn the Slayer."

"And you called me violent. I'm pretty sure that you didn't get that name by rubbing the belly of kittens." He frowned at her and she turned to the other person in the room. She didn't know him either, but his wings were very evident. "How many of you guys are there? I must be having a nightmare again. It's different, I will say that. But this cannot be true."

"In answer to your question, there are as many Protectors as there are beings on this planet. We are paired with one from the moment they are born until they die. When we—"

"So, I'm dead. That man, what's his name?—Goodman. He did kill me, and now I'm having nightmares about— Am I in hell? That would explain a good deal of what I'm going through right now. I mean, winged men are just not real, and the fucking pain in my leg, that's punishment for something I did in my life. Though I tried to be good, perhaps His standards aren't as easy to understand as we all thought." Valyn put his hand over her mouth and she bit down hard. When he jerked his hand back, she could see that she'd drawn blood. "I told you to stop treating me like a child."

"You were babbling, and I only wished to assure you that you are not dead. You are in my home, and you are hurting because I wanted you to wake for a bit." She watched him carefully as he picked up a pill bottle and handed it to her. "The dosage is there for you to see."

"And what do you expect me to do with this? For all I know, this could be cyanide or something to kill me." He growled, and she had to look away. What sort of strange drug was she on that would make her turned on by the sound? "I'd like to be taken to the shelter in town. I know they said that they couldn't take me because of the crutches, but I'll just throw them away when I get there."

"You are the most stubborn and ferocious thinking person I have ever spoken to. You are not going anywhere until I say so." The other man told him to behave. "How should I act when she is forever accusing me of trying to murder her, or that I'm prone to harming her?"

"You act like a man who has just been given a great and priceless gift." Her and Valyn both snorted at the same time. "I can see that my work here is done. I will leave you both here. I would very much appreciate it if you didn't kill each other...no, no, you can no longer do that. Well, the best I can say is, try to remember that once words are said to someone, they will last forever."

He was gone after saying that. Not just like he'd left the room, but he simply disappeared. Jenny closed her eyes and opened them again to see if she'd been mistaken. *Of course*, she thought, *I'm dead, and all sorts of things can happen to a person when they are dead.*

"You are not dead." Jenny didn't even bother looking at him. Whether or not he was right, there was a lot of shit going on that frightened her a great deal. "I could heal you, so that the pain will go away from the gunshot wound. But I fear you will try to leave on your own, and I don't want that."

"So, you'd rather see me in pain? Never mind. Just go away, please. I know you said that this is your home and I shouldn't be ordering you around, but I hurt and I'm sort of sick to my belly again." Closing her eyes, she felt the tears falling from her eyes to her cheeks. When he touched his finger to her forehead, she nearly came up off the bed when the pain was just gone. "What did you do?"

"I didn't want you in pain. I thought we could talk now. If you don't mind." Shaking her head, she bent her leg several times before she laid back on the bed. "See? You are mended. And you no longer hurt, right?'

"No, I don't hurt anymore." She pulled the bandages off her leg, and while the gauze was soaked through with blood, there wasn't even a mark on her leg. "You just touched me and— I wasn't shot, was I? I don't know why you'd go to such an elaborate plan, but I'm not going to let you screw me. Or anything else."

He stood up, and she realized that he was very tall— like well over six feet tall. When his wings opened behind him, she could only stare at the sight he made while the sun shone on his back and through the pretty feathers. When he disappeared like the other man had, Jenny laid back on the bed and wondered what the hell was going on.

"Work. I was at work when this man came in and shot Betty in the head, and fired more rounds in the walls after I ducked down behind the counter. He killed Jimmy. That poor man hadn't done a thing wrong and Mr. Goodman killed him. Then he shot me." That wasn't everything, but she was only hitting the highlights for now. "A man I don't know came to tell me that I was mate to a person named Valyn. Then when I do get away from the hospital, someone, another winged person, picks me up and I throw up then pass out. Now here I am, healed, and wondering what the fuck is going on."

"You usually speak to yourself?" She looked at the woman there and tried to remember her name. "Kala. You met me on the sidewalk just before you were brought here. I've come to answer any questions that you might have. And you'll notice that I'm not cursing. It is one of my better traits, but I'm trying not to scare you anymore."

"Is this for real?" As an answer to her question, Kala pinched her in the arm really hard. "What the fuck, lady, that hurt. Why did you do that?"

"To assure you that one, you're not dead, and secondly, this is all real. I would have thought that being in pain with your wound would have been enough, but you were still unsure. Shall I pinch you again?" Jenny told her no. "Good. What do you have for me?"

"Where am I? I know that I'm in Valyn's home, but where is that? On a different plane or something?" Kala laughed, and Jenny felt her own mouth start to curl up and join her. "You're very lovely. I'm sure that people tell you that all the time, but you really are."

"Thank you. I think that you are beautiful. And you no longer have to lie about in this bed. Here, I've brought you some clothing to put on. I think it will make you more comfortable." Thanking her, Jenny stood up, still cautious about any pain coming to her, and pulled the shirt she had on over her head. "You are very thin, aren't you? I can have Janie make you something to eat and have it ready when we go downstairs."

"Okay. But tell her not to go to any trouble. It's been so long since I've had a full meal, I don't think my belly can take it." She pulled on the jeans and was surprised that they fit her. "It's been a long time since I've had new clothing. I'd tell you that I'll pay you back, but I'm broke and there is little chance that I won't be that way for the rest of my life."

"You don't have to worry about any of that. You're an immortal now. I'll meet you in the dining room when you're ready. There are toiletries on the counter in the bathroom for you too." Kala left her there, heading out the door as she spoke. Jenny sat down hard on the floor.

"Did she just say I was immortal?"

~*~

Valyn wasn't sure that his room would still be his when he'd come back to his place of work. He was positive that Boss knew he was here, but he hoped, just for a bit longer, that he'd leave him alone. He took to his bed and closed his eyes to think.

She was beautiful. Even when she was spitting fire at him, he'd thought her the most beautiful creature ever made. Jennifer. Even her name instilled a calmness over him that he'd not felt in centuries. But she was untrusting, and seemed to have it in her head that someone wanted her dead.

He had already asked Renie to find out what she could about the woman. And there had been plenty. All of it there as a public record, she had told him, but in digging deeper, Renie had found a lot more personal things, things that had taken her to the point she was now.

"There's a charge card that someone took out in her name and charged well over fifty grand on it. Apparently before this happened to her, Jenny had outstanding credit and paid her bills on time. But the credit card company took everything that she had, including her home. She's been living like this for two years now, barely holding on to anything and paying the company most of what she made every month." He had asked her which company. "That's the funny thing. I can't find them."

"I don't understand that. I mean, I know what a credit card is and what its used for, but how can you not find the company?" She turned the computer toward him and let him see what came up when she did a search on Becker Credit Union. All it said was, did she want to buy that name. "So, this company is not in existence anymore. Perhaps they have another —"

"There has never been a company called that. It's a scam, I think." She typed some more keys and turned it back to him again. "This is the transcript of the trial that found her guilty of credit card fraud. After spending four weeks in the county lock up, she was brought before the court again. This time they had payment arrangements for her. She either pays or goes to prison for a long time."

27

"How can they do that?" Renie shrugged and told him that things like that happened a lot more than people knew about. "She's still in debt, correct? She hasn't managed to pay it off, has she?"

"No. She isn't anywhere close to paying it off, Valyn. And at this rate, she never will. They tack on a tax charge every month, which is more than the payments she's making. Instead of going forward on this, she's going backwards every time she makes a payment."

He looked at how much she was paying every month and wondered how she did it. Asking Renie how much she made in a weeks' time, he knew it was much too low for her to make her rent, pay this bill, and eat.

"Usually, I'm betting that she goes without food. Kala told me that she's very thin and malnourished."

And now he had upset her. It hadn't been his intention to do much more than speak to her about being his mate. He wanted her to understand that while she could come to him for money anytime she needed it, he was in no way going to take her as his bride. But when she looked at him, he'd nearly gathered her in his arms and wrapped her in his wings to make her better.

He reached out to her to see what she was doing. She was angry again, and he wondered who was on the other end of her wrath. Smiling to himself, he thought her to be the winner of it should it come to blows. Not that he wanted her to hurt anyone, but she was certainly strong enough to take care of herself.

But that did not mean that he was taking her as his mate. He might be impressed with her, but she would be hurt if she came to him. Valyn wasn't kidding when he said that he was broken. As far as he could tell, he no longer had a heart in his chest. It had stopped beating on a day that he'd never forget.

He had been a protector of a small girl when it had happened, and he could never forgive himself for not paying full attention to her when she was murdered. The man who had murdered her, and so many before little Louisa, had entered the little café and picked her up from her family. What he did to her after escaping everyone's notice had haunted him every day since then.

She'd been kidnapped. Right there, he'd led her away from her parents and younger brother by offering her a bit of chocolate. It had been a favorite of hers, and when she disappeared from Valyn's sight, he found the small chunk of chocolate by the door that the man had taken her out of.

It had been easy for him to find her. They were connected in a way that no one would be able to break but in death. When he'd gotten to her, the man had bound and gagged her and had her lying across his horse. Valyn had tried his best to get her to wake, but the blow to her head had knocked her out soundly. By the time they were at the house, she'd thrown up several times and he had comforted her as best he could.

When she was tied to the bed, his mind was full of things that the man might do to her. And it had been so much worse. She was raped daily, sometimes more than once a day. This went on for two weeks. And Valyn never left her side, encouraging her to think of escaping. To try and get away. Telling her that her mother and father were still looking for her.

Food wasn't given to her unless she performed an act on this man that sickened her and Valyn. But he'd been with her that final day, the day that the monster had taken a large stone from the yard and hit her several times in her little skull with it. He held her hand, sobbing when she took her last breath. The man had gotten another girl and was going to do the same to her. Going to someone else's human, Valyn had told him in great detail what had happened to the child, and that the monster had another. The man was hung a week after they caught him. And the child that he had when he killed Louisa was still alive when they found her.

He had vowed that day that he'd not take another child through a young death, telling Boss that he'd quit him and the Protectors if he had to go through that again. So since then he'd never had to watch a child die as Louisa had. But the images had never left his thoughts.

His door opened with a loud bang, and he sat up to look at Riss when he entered. The blow to his face was unexpected and knocked him back against the wall. Before he could ask Riss what he was doing, he kicked him thrice and told him to get up so he could hit him again.

"No. What are you doing this for? What reason could you have?" He told him that Jenny needed him. "Unless she is being harmed by someone in my house, I don't believe you."

"You left her there." He said that he'd had to. "No, you didn't. You took her to your home, then left her to search out answers on her own. Did you know that she has nothing to fall back on now that she's left your home? Nothing, Valyn."

He started to argue with Riss when something he'd said clicked in his mind. "What do you mean, now that she's left my home?" Riss told him what had happened that had her leaving. "She was safe there. Had food and comfort. Why would she leave such a secure environment?"

"Perhaps because she was left alone in your house and didn't know why she was even there. Or it could be your *charming* personality that made her want to leave. It certainly does make me want to punch you in the face again." Spreading his wings, Valyn asked him how long she'd been gone. "I don't know. I just found out about five minutes before I came here to teach you a lesson. And in this, you have no one to blame for her running but yourself."

"I did nothing to her." Riss told him that was the problem. "I don't understand this. She should have stayed there. Now I will have to find her and bring her back. Where did she go?"

The second punch took him to the floor. He laid there, trying to think why Riss would hit him a second time when he said he'd go and get her, when the other man began talking through clenched teeth.

"You're a fool. A bigger fool than any man that I've ever encountered. You do not order her around like a lost animal; she isn't one. You do not think that you're going out of your way to make sure that she's safe. You do it because she's your world." Valyn said that she wasn't going to be his mate. "It's much too late for that. The moment that you touched her, she became like us. I'm guessing that we'll have to explain that to her as well."

Valyn continued to lay on the floor after Riss left him. He had been a fool. A fool for letting her anywhere near him. He knew what it looked like, but she would be hurt, more so than what the man who had shot her had done. She still had a heart to break, and Valyn was trying his best not to do it.

Getting up, he closed his eyes and searched for Jennifer. When he found her, he started to ask for help in getting her back. But they'd more than likely tell him that he was on his own for doing this, and he left his room for the bar that she was in front of.

"I really don't want a date, but thank you for asking." The man talking to her said that he'd not asked. "I'm well aware of that. I was being sarcastic. I want you all to back off before I have to hurt you. I will too."

She swung her backpack around and clipped one of the four men on the chin. As he was falling down, she rammed her head into the next man's belly. When he bent in half, clutching his belly, she brought her foot up between his legs and hit him right in his manly parts. Not only did he go down as well, but he also puked on the first man that was down.

Man number three that was trying to harm her was taken care of by Valyn. Just a bit of magic sent the man into the bar without a memory of what he'd been doing. Reaching for the fourth man, he grabbed his shoulder at the same time Jennifer screamed at him to leave her alone.

Valyn had no time to react when the backpack came

around and hit him in the head. He went down hard, but was glad to see that the last man had been taken care of too. Wondering if she'd leave him where he was — not that he didn't deserve that and more — he was surprised when she came to sit by him in the snow, and he asked her if she was all right.

"You moron. What are you doing here anyway? I thought that you have better things to do than to yell at me." He told her he was sorry. "Yeah? Well, that doesn't cut it with me. You're a bully and an ass. I'd rather be anywhere but where you are."

When she stood up, he did as well. Wiping at the place where she'd hit him, he saw blood on his fingers. Blood — there was so much of it that it took his mind back to the day. He lashed out quickly, trying to kill the man that had killed Louisa, and fell back when he was hit again.

CHAPTER 3

Galin watched over his friend and tried not to laugh. It wasn't nice, he was aware of that, but when he'd found him, passed out from numerous head wounds, Galin knew Valyn's mate had gotten the better of him. Why, he didn't know, but he was sure he'd find out sooner or later. He looked up when Dusty came in the room with them.

"I put Jenny up in one of the rooms on the lower floor. She's so upset that I don't think this is doing her a bit of good. I couldn't even get her to eat anything. But I didn't tell her that Valyn was here. I don't think that would go over well. What the fuck was he doing hitting her like he did?" Few knew what ate at Valyn. Galin knew only because when he'd knocked him out, Boss had appeared and told him about the child. Galin didn't say anything, not breaking the promise that he'd made to Boss about it. "Galin? What are you not telling me?"

"I can't tell you. It's not mine to tell." Dusty didn't like it, he could tell, but she didn't ask him again. "I don't think he was hitting her. I think that when he saw the blood, like Jenny thought, it had him remembering it from some other time."

"I can see that. I don't like it, but I see it. Jenny had to have ten stitches put in her cheek, as well as she has a concussion. When I gave her the pain pill before coming in here, she didn't even ask what it was but took it and closed her eyes." Galin felt sorry for both of them. For Valyn because he'd carried around the guilt for so long, and Jenny because she was sort of caught in the middle of it. "Galin, do you think this will work out for them?"

"Yes, I don't know why I think that, especially after this, but I'm sure that it will."

He looked down at his friend and shuddered when he thought of what he'd come upon. Valyn had been about to slay his mate with his sword. It was pulled from him to a high arc in the sky when Galin hit him with all that he had. Never in all his lifetimes had he ever hit another person, and he wished that he'd been able to avoid it for a lot longer.

"Will he wake soon? I want to have a word or two with him when he does." Galin laughed. It really wasn't funny, but to see his little slip of a mate taking on a man as large as Valyn was funny to him. But he knew that she'd come out on top. Of that he had no doubt.

"I've never hit anyone before, so I have no way of knowing." She told him he'd done a good job. "You say that, but I'm sure that Valyn won't have the same opinion. I hit him hard. But I was frightened, and in such a hurry to stop him that I didn't think to pull back."

"If he gives you any trouble about it, you let me know. I'll set him straight."

She left him there, and he had to think what he was going to say to Valyn when he woke. It wasn't a question of if he would, but when at this point. He almost regretted him having the headache that he was sure he was going to have.

The next time he glanced in his direction, Valyn was looking at him. Asking him if he was all right, Galin put his hand to his face and told him he was going to be fine. After helping him sit up on the big bed, Galin waited for him to be upset with him. Not that he would blame him for being upset, but Galin wasn't going to let Valyn's mate be killed. That would put him over the edge, Galin knew it.

"Is Jennifer here? I can feel her, but she's not well." He told him that she'd been sedated. "I nearly cut her with my sword. If not for you, I would have."

"I wasn't sure how you'd feel about me hurting you. I'm very sorry, but as you said, you were about to kill her." Valyn told him that she was already an immortal, as he was. "Then I'm doubly glad that I saved her. She would have spent the rest of her days in a wheelchair."

Valyn stood up and so did Galin. When Valyn walked to the window, Galin sat down again. Valyn was hurting, not from the hit to his face but in his heart. Valyn started talking before Galin could tell him again how sorry he was.

"I have no heart to give to her. It's been taken from me." Galin was confused by that statement. Everyone had a heart. "Long ago I let my heart harden until it no longer beat except to keep me alive. Now it is frozen there, beating

37

but closed off from love and any other emotion."

"I don't believe that, and I can't believe that you do. You have the kindest heart that I've ever known. I've seen you with the children here. You are good and kind to them. You have a heart, Valyn. And perhaps it has been frozen for a long time, but I think that Jenny can help you with that."

"No, I don't think I've anything left, Galin. I know that." Galin wasn't sure what to say to him. This was so wrong that he was sure that someone had made a mistake somewhere along Valyn's life. "What will she do should I have another nightmare as I did? You think that you will be there to save her every time it happens? I don't think so. And once she figures out that I'm incapable of loving someone, even her, do you suppose that she'll be all right with that? Maybe tell me that it's not a problem for her? She is a lovely woman, who deserves better than me."

"We'll never know if you don't give her a chance. Or yourself one. What do I tell her when she wakes, Valyn? That you're not here and have gone someplace to sulk? Because that is just what you're doing, sulking like a small child without his treat." Galin wanted to hit him again and leave him where he landed. "I can't believe you, of all people, are doing this to someone that you're supposed to love. Not to mention what you're taking from her because of how you treat her. Neither of you will ever find another person to love you if you leave her. It's a set deal that you and she are a couple. You'll never know the feelings like I have for Dusty. Or the feeling of a woman holding you when you're down. You're taking so much from her, and you don't even care."

"I care a great deal. But I have nothing to offer her." Galin thought of all the things he could say to him, but didn't. His mind was set, and that was all there was to it. "I'll give her money and a place to stay. But I can't mate with her."

"Then you are going to be the unhappiest man alive."

Galin left him then. He didn't want to even be in the same room with him any longer. Making his way down the stairs, he pulled Dusty to him when she asked him if Valyn was awake. He hated that his friend was doing this. Hated it even more when he knew that there was nothing he could do to change his mind.

"I'm going to talk to Jenny when she wakes up. Tell her that she'll have a house to live in and money enough so that she won't be without again. But he won't go to her. He said that he had no heart in him." Dusty pulled away from him a little and stared at him. "I don't know what I'm supposed to do now. She's going to be safe, but she'll never have a man love her like I do you."

Going into the living room, he noticed that Michael was there. Telling him that he wasn't in the mood to talk to him right now, Michael nodded. But he sat down when he did. He didn't have anything to say to him, so he let him speak.

"Jennifer is going to leave here when she can. And I'm going to take away his connection to the girl when she does. He won't be able to find her, no matter what." Galin asked him if that was all right. "He will not love her or give her a chance. It'll be best for them both if they go their separate ways."

"I suppose, but I do worry about Valyn. I can't think
that he's had an easy life. Not for a very long time." Michael
said that he hadn't, that some were not meant for this line
of work. "But he did it for so long. You'd think that we
would have figured that out before now, before it came to
him losing his mate."

"I'll go and talk to him, tell him what I'm going to do.
Perhaps that will motivate him enough that he could see
her once more." Galin didn't think that would work any
better, but didn't say that to Michael. "The young woman,
she is mending well? I heard that he hurt her."

"He did, but she's going to be fine. It wasn't anyone's
fault. He was in a bad place and she tried to help him. I
think he feels worse for it." If he had a heart that was open
for love, Galin supposed that he would.

Michael left him then, and it wasn't long before Galin
heard the shouting. Just Valyn's voice, not Michael's. And
when Valyn came storming into the living room with him,
Galin stood up, ready for anything that he dished out.

"Did you know what he is going to do? He's going to
take my connection from her. What if she's hurt or needs
something?" Galin asked him why he'd care. "I would like
for someone to think how this is affecting me for once. I do
not want her hurt because I can't love her."

"So you say. But I for one am glad that you won't be
able to haunt her. And you will. You'll be near her, without
her knowing, and that will be worse than taking her as a
mate and not loving her." Valyn growled low and full of
menace. "You don't frighten me, Valyn. Not anymore.

You're just a sad man that has nothing left, or so you say."

When Valyn stalked out of the room, he heard him shouting for Jenny. Galin sat down. He'd either find her or he wouldn't. It was out of his hands now. When it got quiet he figured that he'd found her, or his wife had taken him to task and kicked him out of their home. She would do it too.

Getting up when things were just too quiet, he found Dusty standing outside the door to one of the bedrooms. Going to her, he pulled her away from the door and into the kitchen. She told him that Valyn was in the room with Jenny and she was afraid that he'd harm her.

"He won't. I know that with all that I am. He might be cruel to her, but he won't hurt her physically." She told him that wasn't very reassuring. "Yes. I'm sorry, but I don't know what to do either."

"Valyn needs his ass kicked. Several times over. To think that he has the most wonderful person in the world just in front of him, and the fucktard is pushing her away." Galin laughed and Dusty glared at him. "You know that I'm right. He is stupid for thinking that this will end the way he wants it to."

Galin told her what Michael was going to do. "I don't know what that will solve. Not for either of them. But perhaps she'll be able to find someone to care for her someday."

Galin had to go to work, and he knew that Dusty was missing a few things as well. So he helped her get ready to leave and told her that it would be all right. Not that he really thought it would, but he thought that something would happen if they were there or not.

"I don't have to like this." Galin told Dusty that he didn't like it either. "I won't be surprised if we come home and there is a blood bath in that room. And it will be Valyn that will be the one hurt. He's a fucktard. I'm telling you that in case I haven't before."

"You have. Perhaps you should come up with a better word. Or a different one." She smiled at him. "Maybe not. You have a vocabulary of curse words that somewhat scares me."

"I'm going to work on it. Just for you. I have a list of curse words that I can combine to make new ones. I think I'll take the list with me and work on it between jobs." He kissed her on the nose. "I love you, Galin."

"And I you, Dusty."

They left for work at the same time. He had three meetings to go to this morning and two more after lunch. They were going to work on a couple of projects as a family, and he was in charge of getting stats they might need. This was the part of working that he loved most. Figuring things out.

~*~

Valyn watched her sleep. He was sure that she needed it, but he also wanted to make sure that she was all right. Reaching down to touch the small curl that laid on her cheek, he was astounded by how silky it was. Caressing her skin under it, thinking no one would be the wiser, he felt first her warmth and then the softness of her skin.

She rolled to her back and he yanked his hands away. He'd been about to pull her hair from the stretchy thing she had it in. Valyn was sure that it was curly everywhere,

42

but without ever seeing her with her hair down, he wanted to make sure.

He ran his finger over her nose to her lips. The soft puffs of air that passed them was warm and smelled of mint. Leaning closer, just to get a better whiff, he told himself, Valyn did something that he'd never thought of doing before. He brushed his lips over hers.

It was overwhelming, the feeling and taste of her. Valyn had expected her mouth to be warm, but not that it'd be beautiful as well. Sitting up so that he could look at her face while he touched her hair, he wondered what it would be like to have someone look at him the way Dusty and the other women looked at their mates.

Glancing at her hair again, he marveled at the shades in it. To say that it was brown would be criminal. It was all the colors that he'd ever seen. Browns, yes, but there was yellow like the daffodils in the spring. There were reds too, like the first roses that came up in the middle of the summer. He thought it strange that he also saw other colors, a blueish color as well as some green. He would have to ask her about that—

She was looking at him. He jerked back like she'd hit him and started to rise. But she put her hand on his arm and asked him to stay. He could have left, he knew that, should have really, but he sat back down for her.

"You're all right now, aren't you?" He was, he told her. "Good. I was worried about you when you seemed to have buzzed out for a bit. You have some very terrible dreams and thoughts, don't you?"

"I do. I watched a small girl be brutalized by a man

who had kidnapped her. Day after day for a week he hurt her, both with his fists and sexually. Then, while I watched helplessly, he killed her with a stone that was lying nearby." She sat up, and he was still trying to wrap his mind around the fact that he'd told her. Just like that. "It has haunted me for a great many years. More than it should have, but—"

"No, don't say that. It was terrible, and you have to heal from it." Valyn nodded but didn't tell her that he never would. "Is that why you said you have no heart to give me?"

"Yes, I have come to hate people from that." She nodded and touched her fingers to the bruise that he knew was there. "I cannot love you, Jennifer."

"My grandmother was the only person in the world that called me Jennifer. She was a nice woman, sort of stern, but her rules were wonderful to me. My parents had been lax in their raising me. They left me with her more often than not. Not that I cared. She was wonderful." Valyn knew who her grandmother was. And her watcher. He let Jennifer turn his face so that she could look at the damage done to him. "You were so angry when you drew your sword. I knew that you weren't seeing me when you did, and I wasn't afraid of you cutting me. You were hurting, and I could see that."

"I hurt a great deal." She let his face go and he turned to look at her again. "Your hair, it has strange colors in it. I don't understand that."

Her laugh nearly took him to his knees. It was soft and tingled like a small bell. He watched her face as she smiled at him, and Valyn felt something stir within his chest. He rubbed the place where his heart had been and wondered what was wrong with him.

"I had my hair done at the college that teaches men and women how to cut and style hair. It was free, and I so needed a haircut. But when she was finished, I was astounded by the colors too." She grinned an impish sort of smile at him. "I don't know if she passed the test or not, but the next time I need a haircut, I'm going someplace that I have to pay for."

"Don't cut it." She asked him why. "It's lovely. Soft too. Much softer than I thought it to be. And the small colors are beautiful in it. I'm not thinking that you'd look good with those colors everywhere, but it suits you now. Sort of like you have a flair for yourself that no one can see until they are close enough."

"Thank you." Nodding at her, he took her hand into his much larger one and felt the calluses on them. There were small scars on her fingers, some of them old, most of them fresh. "Sometimes I'd have to cut tomatoes to help out. Jimmy would...he would tell me how many to cut, and it was always too much. But he gave them to me at the end of my shift. That way I could have something substantial with my bread and water."

"You were shot that day. He nearly killed you." Valyn could hear the tenderness in his voice and wondered about that. "He killed one woman and one man. The cook."

"Yes. Jimmy was calling the police. I think that's why they were there so quickly. The lady, I don't know her name, she was just sitting there, minding her own business, and he killed her." Jennifer looked up at him, sadness in

45

her beautiful eyes. "I don't want to talk about that. I know that I should, that's what the doctor told me, but it's all so raw for me."

"There was not that sort of advice when I had my trauma. I know that I wasn't hit or killed, but the child had come to mean a lot to me. They all do, but she was special." She asked him if he wanted to talk about it now. "Yes. I want you to know why I can't love you."

"I don't expect anyone to love me, Valyn. I know that I'm just short of being white trash. And when I leave here, and I will, I'll live on the streets. It's not that difficult for me. I've done it before." Valyn told her that he had a house and money that he wanted her to have. "No — thanks, but no. It would feel like you were paying me off, which I'm guessing you are. But I would feel dirty taking it from you."

When she stood up, he did as well. There were more tears in her eyes, and he had a feeling that they were shed for him. She picked up a small bag that looked to have clothing in it and turned back to him. With a short wave, she was out the door.

"Why are you just sitting here?" He'd not heard Michael come in, he'd been so lost in thought. "Did you hear what she said? She's going to live on the streets. Have you no compassion at all, Valyn?"

"She's more than likely going to bounce back from this. She's strong, and I pity the man that tries to mess with her." The pain in his chest had him rubbing it. "Why are you here? Did Boss tell you to come and make me marry her?"

"Nay, Valyn, I'm here to take her from your memories."

He just stared at his friend. "We both know that you cannot survive without having her near you. I've discussed what would happen should you turn away from this. I've not come to blackmail you into it, but to simply rid you of her memories and scent. You will no longer be able to find her."

He leapt back when Michael came toward him. The thought of not remembering anything about her hurt him again. He shook his head at Michael when he said it was for the best.

"What do you know of what is best for me? To not remember the feel of her flesh beneath my fingers would wound me. The memory of the feel of her hair when it curled around my fingers is all that I have. I will not allow you to do this." Michael pointed out that those things shouldn't matter because he didn't love her. "No. I won't allow you to do that to us. To me."

He left the room, bypassing Michael and his sword before he could touch him. Valyn needed to find her. All he could think about was finding Jennifer right now. But where to look?

Lifting himself to the sky, he closed his eyes and reached for her. Just the touch of her skin was enough for him to know where she might be. But it wasn't enough for him to speak to her. When he saw the place that she had gone, he went to her. She was just where he had felt her, walking along the road that led to town. Picking her up in his arms as he dove over her, her scream startled him. Then the laughter made his heart—yes, he realized almost too late that it was his heart—feel good.

Landing on the roof of his home—their home—he

didn't immediately put her down. She felt wonderful in his arms. Like she had belonged there since he'd been created. Leaning toward her, he brushed his mouth over hers once, then a second time before he lifted his head to look at her.

"I've been a fool." She said that he had been. He laughed at her honesty. "You will keep me in line, I think. I was accused recently of pouting. I think that you will not allow that anymore."

"No. If you do this—if we do this, there will be rules." He nodded and watched her mouth as it moved. The way her tongue moistened her lips a little. When he felt the pain in his ear, he looked at her. "Are you paying any attention to me? I was telling you the rules that we'll have."

"I will do them all. Wait, I don't know what you said, but I was paying attention. You have lovely lips; did you know that? And a small nose with a tiny scar just on your left nostril." She told him that she'd had it pierced once but it hurt too much, and she took it out. "I want to know everything about you. I will tell you what haunts me as well. You'll be there for me. You love me."

"Yes." He looked at the sadness that came over her face and asked her what was wrong. "Nothing. I think I've loved you since you came into my life."

Reaching gently into her mind, he found the reason for her sadness and again, he felt the fool. Taking her hand into his, he got down on one knee and looked up at her. This right here was going to make him better; he could love her.

"Will you marry me, Jennifer? Be my wife, my partner in all things. Before you answer that, I'd like to tell you something important. I love you. I love you with all my beating heart, and I will forever." She started to cry and told him that was a lovely declaration. "I mean it. Without you my heart would have stayed closed up until I would have to be put to rest. This time it would have been longer than a decade. Will you be with me for the rest of your life and mine?"

"Yes."

The air around them seemed to pick up. He knew what was about to happen and pulled her into his arms as he stood up. Wrapping his wings around them both, he knew the moment that they stood in the office of Boss.

"It's about time." Valyn laughed with Boss and said that he was a moron. "Well, I'd not say that, but you did take your time about things. I'm glad though. Going into this without a heart, it would have been terrible for you both. Now, let me wed you."

The rings fit them like they'd been made just for them. He could feel the magic that was in his, the way it glowed because of the tears of the man he loved. After Boss pronounced them man and wife, he was able, finally, to kiss his bride.

CHAPTER 4

She was nervous. Jenny had never had sex before, and Valyn had told her that he hadn't either. She could hardly believe that; a man as delicious as him would have had women all over him. But he explained to her that while he was around a great many women, none of them could see him.

"But there was never anyone that I saw as beautiful as you are at this moment." She smiled at him. "I have a hot tub outside of our doors. Would you like to relax in it? I have yet to use it, fearful of not wanting to ever come out of it again."

"I thought we'd have sex." Her face heated up. She sounded like a sex crazed woman, which she supposed she was. "I didn't mean that the way it came out. I'm very nervous."

"So am I. But we'll muddle through this. Come on, the water is very warm, and it has bubbles." He sounded like a child then, and she let him guide her to the outside porch that was only theirs. When he slipped into the steaming water and moaned, she almost begged him to take her right now.

Getting in for her was trickier than she thought it was for him. First of all, the side that she was trying to get in on was too high for her to just put her leg over it. The second thing was, she didn't know how to swim. Not that she'd drown or anything, but water scared her.

Valyn came to her rescue and lifted her up and put her in the water with him. On his lap. Where he was very hard and manly. She nearly giggled at how she sounded, and thought of the kiss he'd given her in the office. Leaning down to him, she kissed his chin, then his cheeks. Jenny wanted to explore every part of him while she could.

"Do I get to do this to you?" He turned her around so that she was facing him, his cock so hard between her legs. "Please don't stop. I'm enjoying this a great deal."

Starting over, she nipped this time, then kissed the tiny hurt that she made. His hands were busy too, and she moaned when he cupped her breasts in his hands. When he tugged on her nipple with his teeth, Jenny thought that her eyes had rolled around in her head several times before coming to a stop.

"The way you're sitting on me makes me want to take you now." She nodded against his neck and moaned again when he lifted her up. "I'll be careful with you, Jennifer, but I have a sudden need that I feel you're the only one that can fulfill."

His cock was at her entrance, and she wanted him too. Valyn did take care with her, lowering her over him slowly. When she felt her virginity break, Valyn brought her down hard and she felt ripped apart. The scream torn from her seemed to come from her feet and back.

When she thought that she could move, Jenny realized that he was speaking to her. He was telling her how sorry he was, that he'd never hurt her again. That he would flay his skin off if he did. Lifting his head from her breast as he held her tightly, she kissed him on the mouth and moved.

Jenny rode him. His body was hard and felt good under her fingers as she held onto him. She had a feeling that if she was able to come, she'd be broken apart into tiny fragments and never be the same afterward.

The water was splashing out now, and she thought about telling him to take her inside, but he raised her up and laid her on the deck while his cock was still deep inside of her. Nothing could have prepared her for the new sensation that she was feeling. The way that something inside of her was building. She wrapped her legs around his waist, and he lifted her foot up to kiss her on the calf.

"You are mine." She told him that she was, forever. "I will never harm you again, not by my hand or my words. You are the greatest gift I never thought to have."

"Take me, Valyn. I ache to come with you."

He leaned toward her then, taking her breast into his mouth. When he bit down on her hard, and she was sure breaking her skin, she came so hard that she saw rainbows and stars just before he threw back his head and roared at his own release. Jenny was spent, her body too limp to move. She didn't care if she ever did, and she closed her eyes.

When she woke, not only was she in bed, but Valyn was there as well. He was looking at her, and she had a feeling that he'd been doing it for some time. Moving on the bed so that she could get a better glimpse of him, she smiled when he kissed her and rolled over top of her.

"I'm running late, but I couldn't help but look at you again and again." She asked him where he was going. "Riss called me, through our link, and said that he needed me on the field today for a few hours. Then I'm coming back here to make love to you again."

"I like that idea." Sitting up, she winced at the pain in her body. Valyn noticed it and told her that he could heal her. "Can I do that too?"

"Not yourself. That has repercussions that will make you wish that you hadn't. But there are things you can do. I'm sure you've been told about a few of them. Like the one I use most is dressing myself without thought to what I need to wear." She told him that was her favorite too. "I have to go."

"You said that, but here you still are. The sooner you leave, the sooner you can get back here to me." He kissed her again and got off the bed with her. When he stood in the bedroom and looked around, she did as well. "Something wrong, Valyn?"

She didn't see anything out of the ordinary, but she didn't know a great deal about magic. When he turned to look at her, she thought that he was the most beautiful man she'd ever seen. Snapping his fingers, he had a handful of cash and gave it to her.

"What do you think I'm going to do with all this?"

There had to be fifty one hundred dollar bills, plus some lower denominations. "This is a great deal of money. Am I going to be arrested for having counterfeit money?"

"Nay, it's mine — ours. I worked for a long time and never bought much of anything. This house, I've had it for a few centuries, and over the years, I would update it or paint something. But it was never anything that I enjoyed. The house I mean. And I know why now. It's not homey." She laughed at him and asked how homey he wanted it. "Whatever it takes. I wish for you to make this a home for us."

Then he disappeared. But before she could begin to miss him, he was back and kissed her soundly on the mouth. After he left the second time, she waited for a few moments to see if he'd return, and when he didn't, she went to take a shower.

The whole house was heaven for her. There were rooms that were bigger than her tiny place before coming here. And they were set up with the most beautiful antiques, more beautiful than any she'd seen in catalogs. Even the master bathroom, with all its beauty, was big enough for several people to be standing in it.

After thinking about what to wear, she opted for comfy with a pair of jeans and a T-shirt, then made her way down to the kitchen. Janie was just pouring tea into a pitcher when she entered the room.

"Good morning, miss." She told her the same. "I don't know a great deal about you, so I made you a sample breakfast. If there is anything you don't like, you tell me, and I'll cut it from the menu, so to speak."

There was so much food on the large platter that she looked at Janie once again. "Is someone joining me for breakfast? Perhaps an army of hungry men?" She laughed so that Janie would know she was joking, and she could see the relief on her face. "I'm not used to having people work for me. I'm sort of new to this having money thing. There is a great deal I'm not used to, but this servant thing—that is what you're called, correct? Well, this servant thing is a little overwhelming."

"Servant is fine, miss. Or you could just call me Janie. That's what Valyn calls me. Did he tell you how I came to be here?" Jenny told her that he had, and was glad that she'd not been wrapped up in the robberies. "I am too. To think he was doing that right under everyone's noses. I'm very glad to be out of there, to be honest. This job, cooking for someone, has been my dream for a very long time."

Jenny tasted the food on the platter. The only thing she didn't care for was the cantaloupe. There were other fruits on the platter as well, and she loved the strawberries most of all. Janie took notes while she ate, and laughed with her when she moaned about the taste of some of the things.

After eating and talking to Janie about food to fix for them, she didn't know what to do with herself. Wandering into the living room, she was startled to see Boss there. He was enjoying a cup of tea and some scones. He asked her to have a seat.

"I have a favor to ask of you." She told him that she wasn't all that talented at much. "You are very talented in a great many things. Never let anyone tell you differently. But this favor, it has to do with the surgery, or hospital if you wish. It seems like such a mundane job, but I promise you, the people that you'll interact with will be much happier for you talking to them."

"Now talking I can do." He laughed when she did. "What do you need me to do? I was just thinking that I don't have a job or anything to do to occupy my time wisely. The other women do, I know, but I'm not very good at combat. I don't like pain. Or inflicting it."

"Understandable. But the job. You would be handing out books to those that wish to read them. Flowers when they are brought in. It's a good job, and I think you'd be perfect at it. You will brighten their days much like you helped Valyn." She told him that she loved Valyn, it had been easy to help him. "And he loves you. I've never — well, not for many years have I seen him smiling as he is today. Nor did I remember that he likes to whistle. I have you to thank for that."

"No thanks are necessary. As I said, I love him. But I will do the job for you. I can speak several languages too, so I can help those that don't speak English." He nodded, and she realized that he'd already known that. Embarrassed again, she changed the subject. "Dusty and the other women are looking into the credit card that I'm paying on. I guess I knew that everyone would know about it, but they didn't have to go to any trouble for me. I had a fair trial, I suppose, and I was found to have taken it out and spent the money. I don't know who might have done this to me, but I guess it's all water under the bridge now."

"They'll find out for you. Just you wait and see." She smiled at him, loving the man for being so kind to her. "All right. You show up at the hospital first thing tomorrow and they'll be ready for you. I cannot wait to see the faces on the people whose lives you touch in doing this."

When he left her, she decided that she couldn't stay in the house any longer. Picking up the phone, she realized that she had no idea what anyone's number was. Frustrated, she thought about Renie and how much she liked her.

Hello, Jenny. The voice in her head startled her. *I'm assuming that since you seem to be frightened a little, no one told you about this magic that you have. You can talk to any of us now. Just do what you did and think of one of us, and we'll be there for you.*

I was going to call to see if you'd like to go shopping with me. I know that it's probably not your usual thing to do, but I don't have a car and I hate driving in the snow. This was much nicer than the phone would have been, Jenny thought. She could even feel her emotions about the idea of shopping with her. Renie *wanted* to spend time with her. *I can be outside if you don't want to come up the driveway.*

You most certainly will not. You'll wait in the warm house until we come and get you. She smiled at the sternness of her voice. Renie, like the other women, had a mouth on her that would make her blush at times. *This is perfect. We had a lunch planned that you were going to come to anyway. Now we can make a day of it. The rest of them are happy to go too. We'll be there in a bit.*

Someone that loved her. A shopping spree. Friends. And money. Jenny wasn't sure she ever wanted to wake from this dream if it was one. She was as happy as she'd ever been. Thinking of a coat, she was dressed warmly when the knock at the door came. Jenny was ready to have some fun.

~*~

"Someone is digging around in that credit card company again. They won't find anything but dead ends, but I thought you'd like to know." Samuel Mercer looked up from the application he was filling out in someone else's name. "Here are the names and socials I was able to get from downtown. There are a few of them on there that could be fun picking out. None of them have much, but they'll be found guilty the same as the rest of them were."

They both laughed, and Betsy Whitaker kissed him on the mouth when she went by him to the filing cabinet. This was the best scam that he'd ever done. And it was also turning out to be the most profitable.

"I have four more applications filled out for you to mail. I even put a little mustard on one of them to make it look like they did it from their own kitchen table." He looked at them and laughed again when he saw that he'd misspelled the street name on one of them. He'd just leave it too. It looked better than being perfect. "When are you going to close up the Boseman Credit Union? I've seen where a few of those people are taking this to court. Won't do them a bit of good—we've already moved on. And the one before that was...let me see. Ah yes, Becker Credit Union. However, I want to be ready to start up the next one. I'm calling it Harney Institute and Trust. What do you think?"

"You're writing these down, aren't you? I'd hate to mess up at this point by calling us the same name we used before." He showed her the sheet of paper that he'd written on in neat order. "Good. I knew that you'd think of that before I did. Oh, there hasn't been a check from two people. I have their names right here. One is Jennifer Hale—she is supposed to pay four hundred a month. Then there is Ashley Knisley. Hers isn't so large of a pay off as the Hale girl is, but still a hundred bucks a month is a hundred bucks."

"Do you have phone numbers for them?" Betsy handed him her notes that were messy and out of order. After finding the two phone numbers, Samuel handed it back to her. He'd have to work on it if he laid it on his desk. "I'll call them around dinner time. That's always good for a laugh or two."

After finishing up another application from Harney Institute and Trust, he picked up the phone to call the women. They were such easy targets, he'd come to realize. Most of them were dumber than a post, and probably crying in their beds at night.

Talking to Ashley first, he giggled when she started sobbing about how she just couldn't make the payment any more. She'd lost her job, and there wasn't any money to spare for her kid's dinner.

"I'm sure that is all fine and good, but you did make the charges on that credit card, and the courts told you to pay us every month so that you don't go to jail. Who do you think is going to feed your children if you're in a cell, far away from them?" She sobbed more and said that she'd figure something out soon. "See that you do. And there will be a late charge attached to next month's bill. Have a nice day."

Next he tried to call Jennifer, but the number that they had was not a working number. And when he called directory assistance to find out what she'd done, he was given an area code that he'd never seen before. He just knew that little bitch had skipped town.

"The Slayer residence." He thought that he'd gotten the wrong number and started to hang up. "Hello? Who is it you're trying to reach? Perhaps I can help you."

"I was calling for Jennifer Hale. I don't suppose you know where I can find her, do you?" The man told him to hold on. After a few minutes, the man came back and told him that Jennifer Slayer was out for the day, and he didn't know when to expect her. "I was looking for Jennifer Hale, not Slayer. I think I have the wrong number, so—"

"I do believe that is her maiden name, so you do have the right number. But as I said, she is out for the day and I don't know when she'll return. Can I take a message for her?" Samuel thought about leaving his phone number—it was a burner phone anyway—and decided what the fuck, she'd never know where he was by that.

After the man repeated his message back to him, Samuel hung up. She had money, it seemed. And a great deal of it if the butler's voice was any indication. He had a rich snob tone in every syllable. Leaning back in his chair, he decided to have himself a little fun. Pulling up a search engine, he put in her maiden name as well as her married name. He got several hits immediately.

She'd married very well, it seemed. The announcement in the paper said that they were residing in the husband's home town. That made Samuel very happy. They were only a short drive away from him. There was no point in sending her another notice; he'd just go see the woman and demand full payment now. And if she didn't have it, well, he'd call the police on her.

He made a list of things that he wanted to say, and things that he'd need to have with him in the event that he had to call the police on her. There really wasn't much that he thought he'd need to prove that she'd been charged with credit card fraud. But, just in case, he took along the application that he'd used to get the supposed credit card.

There were never any charges on the card. Hell, there wasn't even a card to charge against. It was all phony. Just a scam, a good scam that he and Betsy had come up with when she'd been charged with the same thing. However, the difference was, there had been charges and Betsy had made them. They'd had a very good time with that card too.

When Betsy returned several hours later, he had a good list going, as well as how much money they'd need. It had to be gotten out of the safe that was in the basement of their home. No banks for them, no sirree. A bank would want information that neither of them wanted to give. Like their names, for one thing.

Betsy was a wanted criminal. She'd not only murdered her husband several years ago, but she had burned their home down with him still in it. That had all sorts of charges going along with it, some he didn't understand even today.

He too was a wanted man, but his crime wasn't murder, but armed robbery. He and his brother had robbed the First National Bank and Harold had killed a cop. Harold had been shot too, and later died from his injuries. Of course, Samuel had helped him along on that, but it was his fault for getting shot in the first place.

They weren't nice people, he thought with a laugh. And they never claimed to be either. Betsy was as mean as a rattlesnake when she was upset, that was why he did all the phone calls for them. She was better at paperwork. There wasn't much that would piss her off there.

"When do you want to leave here? I'm thinking that we should take our time, let her think that we've forgotten about it." He told Betsy that he'd called and left a message. "That's good. Now if she only calls us back. Do you think she will?"

"I wouldn't. And the fact that she's also skipped town on us means that she's not thinking of anything but what is good for her. They have money too." She asked him how he knew that. "I don't have their address, it only says here what town they live in, but a butler answered the phone. That's how I found out that she'd married."

Betsy sat down and stared at him. She wasn't really staring at him but thinking. It had freaked him out before he figured out that was what she was doing. Her eyes went all blank and her face went lax. She looked like she was dead, she was so still. He also knew never to touch her when she was in this state. He'd been hit before, badly, when he'd tried to get her to wake up.

After about thirty minutes of her staring off, she finally looked at him. That was another thing that had freaked him out about this thing she did. She knew things that he would never think of.

"You'll need to get your suit dry cleaned to make a good impression. These people have money, so we want to flash it around that we do too. For all we know, we could be much more fortunate than them, and we don't want to piss them off from the start. You know how the rich snobs can be. I'm so glad that we're not at all like that. Also, you'll need to have everything you're going to use with you the first time you go see them. You might not get a second chance." He made notes while she spoke in her eerie kind of voice. "A limo won't be too much — it'll show that we have class. I'll book it for us now."

While she was gone, he put all the things he'd gathered up in his briefcase. She'd not told him about that, but he thought it might look more professional when they got there. He went to their bedroom to get his suit to have it cleaned.

Samuel thought this was going to be epic. Confront the girl where there were people around to embarrass her. To him, that was the ultimate insult, to be embarrassed by those that might have respect for you. Not that he knew all that many people who had any kind of respect for him. But he really didn't give two shits if they did or not. He was happy. And he was rich.

CHAPTER 5

Jenny hadn't dressed up for her first day on the job. Michael had told her, late last night, that the people she would be helping would not be as friendly to her if she was dressed to the tens. After correcting him that it was to the nines, she decided to wear something she wore all the time. Jeans and a shirt.

So she had loaded up the cart they'd given her, plus the small chocolates and mints she was told she could hand out, and was on her way. Jenny was also armed with a list, which included names of the people who might need some cheering up, and who was still recovering. There was also a list of the diabetics on the floor. She might not have thought of that.

"Hello. I was wondering if you had any books on building a bomb?" Jenny wasn't sure what she should tell the man, and must have looked very shocked. His laughter made her realize that he'd been joking. "I'm sorry. But you should have seen your face. What sort of things do

65

you think I could do with a bomb, dear? I've been in this wheelchair longer than I was able to walk. I would like a mystery if you have one."

"Yes, we have several." She helped him get one of the books and told him that she could get the series for him if he liked that one. Jenny had an endless supply of books, she'd been told, and could ask for and get the ones that she didn't have. "This is one of my favorite authors. He writes a good chiller that makes you want to sleep with the lights on for about a week after you're done with it."

"Oh, I like a good chiller. Yes, I'll take this one. You're new here, aren't you?" She told him it was her first day. "Don't let some of the people here run over you. There are a couple of them that'll keep you in their room all day, just talking about nothing."

She thought about pointing out that he was doing the same, but he turned in his chair and rolled away. But she was having so much fun just talking to people that she didn't care how long she let them talk.

When she entered the next room on her list, she could smell impending death. Jenny wasn't sure that was actually what it was, but when she entered, she could see three Protectors in the room. That was new to her, seeing them when she knew that no one else could. Nodding to them, she asked the people sitting in the chairs if she could give them a little break, that she'd not mind at all to sit with the woman in the bed for a little while.

"Oh, that would be lovely. I just need to stretch my legs a bit. And Mom, she's so ill right now, I do hate to leave her. But I need to walk." Jenny told her that she'd be right there when they came back.

As soon as they were out the door, she looked at the three with her.

"You can see us." She nodded at the man who spoke. "I'm Tholan, this is Peter and James. They're watching over Ms. Jackson for her final breaths."

"Do you always come to them?" He told her not usually, but she was a special client. "I'm new to this. Valyn is my husband."

"Ah yes, I should have known. I was told that you'd be here today. Welcome." She thanked Tholan and peered down at the woman. "She is near her end of this life. I'm here to take her beyond this realm to make sure that she has special treatment. Her works have saved a great many children, and she's helped a lot of motherless children make a mark in the world."

"She won't pass while I'm here, will she? I mean, I won't mind being here when she does, but I think her family needs to be here, don't you think?" Tholan told her that they'd be back in plenty of time, and thanked her for giving them this rest. "I could see that they were exhausted. How long have they been here with her?"

"They've never left her side since she was brought in five days ago. The daughter, the one that spoke to you, she's carrying on her mother's works, and for that we are grateful. The other woman is someone that had come to mean a great deal to Ms. Jackson. She was the first child that she helped get out of a terrible situation."

"I'm glad that I got to see her then." Jenny took her hand in hers and kissed the back of it. "Go in peace, Ms.

Jackson. Everyone here loves you very much."

Feeling silly that she'd spoken to the woman, Jenny backed away from the bed. But Tholan told her to stay, to hold her hand a bit longer. She took her frail hand in hers again and thought about telling her a story. Even if she couldn't make out what she was saying, she wanted her to hear a voice, so she'd know that she wasn't alone.

"When I was just a little girl, my mother and I used to go to this big department story to look at the displays. At Christmas time it was beautiful." She thought of how angry her mom would be when people stared at them, and then she'd take it out on her. But she didn't tell Ms. Jackson that part. "There was a giant tree in the middle just as you walked in. It was decorated with all sorts of things. Little gifts that sparkled under the lights. Candy canes that were as big as my arm. And there were dolls and trucks, just like a child would imagine their own tree would look like."

Jenny realized that the family was back and stood up to leave. The daughter hugged her tightly and thanked her. Jenny started for the door, just as her eyes filled with tears.

"No, child, tell her the story. Her time here isn't long, but we know that she can hear us. Go on."

She settled on the bed again, taking the warm frail hand into hers again. There were small scars on her fingers, age spots on the back of it. This was a woman who did for herself, and damn what others thought, Jenny imagined. So she changed her story around a bit.

"That year for Christmas, there was only one thing that I wanted. It was a dolly that I could sleep with. One that had soft yellow hair and eyes that closed and opened.

There would be a bottle too, so I could feed her." She had dreamed of that dolly for weeks. But it cost too much, and she didn't get it or anything that year, or any Christmas. "We were very poor — my mother told me that things like dolls were low on the list of things that we could afford. But she did the best she could and had one made for me. It was soft and cuddly, just as I wanted."

All lies, she told herself. Her mother hadn't gotten her anything. The lady that lived in the car next to theirs had given her the one she carried around until it was in tatters and no longer soft. But she was happy for the ending she gave the lady, and kissed the back of her hand again and left the room. She was nearly all the way down the long hall when she heard the room number being called over the intercom. Jenny knew then that Ms. Jackson had died.

The rest of the morning and well into the afternoon, she handed out books, gave away small bits of candy to those that could have them, and fruit snacks to those that couldn't. The list that she'd been given by the charge nurse had been a great help on a lot of things. And she talked to everyone who spoke to her.

By the time she was finished, she was exhausted, both mentally and physically. She had no idea how nurses did it all day long and were able to come back to work the next day. Jenny supposed it took a special kind of person to become a nurse — one that had a heart of gold, but was strong enough to watch those who passed. And compassion for people that few had nowadays.

Pulling on her coat, she was in the main lobby when she saw Valyn. Just what she needed. A man that loved her and strong arms to hold her. As she let him tell her about his day, she held tightly to him, knowing that she couldn't live without him if it came to pass.

"I understand that you helped with a passing today." She looked up at him and told him what she'd done. "Yes, that's what James told me when he took his break today. He told me how you spoke to Ms. Jackson and put her at peace. She could hear you, did you know that?"

"I only wanted to help her family out—you know, give them a little break. And she was just lying there, with all these monitors attached to her. I don't know why I started telling her that story—hardly any of it was the truth. I sort of feel bad that I did that." He said that it was wonderful that she had. "I'm not sure that Tholan thought so. He's sort of stern, isn't he? Not unkind, but very strict, I guess you'd call it."

"He is. And a little out of touch with humans. We try our best to get him to relax more, but he's very stern, as you said."

They were nearly to the car when she saw Boss standing next to it. She wondered if the man ever wore anything that wasn't jeans and a T-shirt. "He would like to speak to you. And before you ask, no, you're not in trouble."

Walking to him, she could see his smile. The man had the kind that would light up the world, she thought. When he pulled her to him and gave her a great bear of a hug, she burst into tears. It was too much today, and it only just then hit her.

"There, there, my child. You're all right now." She nodded, and he lifted her chin up so that she could see him.

"What you did today was well beyond what I would have asked you to do. I'm very proud of you. And you should know that Ms. Jackson loved that you, a stranger, took the time to come and talk to her."

"I feel so bad. It was a lie. Most everything I said to her was a lie. But I thought, why would she want to hear that my mother hated shopping, and hated Christmas even more? And there wasn't a doll for me — nothing, as a matter of fact." He kissed her on the forehead. "You are okay with that?"

"I am. For you didn't do it out of selfish reasons, you did it because you felt the pain of someone you knew wasn't long for this world. You made her happy in her final hour, and that is all we can hope for when someone we love passes from this place to the next." She nodded. "Now, I have a gift for you. You might think it silly, but it's something that I think — I hope — you'll enjoy as much as I did trying to find it."

The package he handed her was in red and green paper, the bow as big as her head. Opening the card that was on the top, she cried a little when she read who it was from. Boss and Ms. Jackson. Jenny had a feeling that she knew just what it was.

The doll was just what she'd wanted that year. Her hair was as bright yellow as the sun, and her dress, a calico, had a pocket with her bottle in it and bloomers under it. Holding it to her, she thanked Boss several times as she wiped at tears. When strong arms wrapped around her from behind, she leaned on Valyn.

"She wanted me to tell you thank you." Jenny nodded,

unable to speak around the emotions that seemed to be stuck in her throat. "Ms. Jackson also said to tell you to never be afraid to do what you did today. It's not so much for the family, but for the dying that will appreciate someone being compassionate to them as you were."

Nodding to him, returning the hug that he gave her, she got into the car with Valyn when Boss left them. Today was her first day of many, she thought, and it had been a great day. She looked at Valyn when he cleared his throat.

"How about dinner, a movie, then home to make passionate love for the rest of the night? I was thinking pizza." She burst out laughing when he wiggled his brows at her. The man simply loved that food, with everything under the kitchen sink on top of it. "I might even be persuaded to let you order your own so that you don't have to eat anchovies again."

"Yuck, yes I will. How can you eat those things?" He was driving now, to the little restaurant that she'd heard served the best pizza in town. It wasn't saying much, as the town didn't even have a grocery store. And only a single stoplight. But she was growing to love the place—mostly the people in it.

The restaurant wasn't busy — it was a Monday evening, after all—so they were seated right away and given their drinks. Almost as soon as they got their drinks, a man came from the back and headed to their table. Jenny knew right away he was a Protector. Or had been one at one time.

She was introduced to the man and hugged. They were very huggy, this group of people. Carter told her that he'd been here on this realm for nearly two hundred years. To her that sounded like a great deal, but she knew that he was more than likely much older than he looked.

"And in that time, I learned a few things about making a good pie. Lots of practice and failures." She laughed when he did. "You enjoy your night. And thank you, Valyn, for bringing your lovely mate in to meet me. It's a pleasure to see you so happy too."

When he was gone, she asked Valyn how many of their kind were around here. "There are a great many of us that are only here to take a break for a time. Once one of our charges pass on, we come here to regroup and to be among the living for a time." He looked around the room and she did as well. "You can see them now, can't you? The Protectors that are with the humans."

"Yes. I didn't know I could do that until today at the hospital."

Jenny watched as one of them leaned down to the elderly man and whispered in his ear. When he picked up the small child next to him, held him close to his heart, she wondered if he was passing soon.

"He is not long for here, no. Sometimes we know when the time is near, but there are times when we haven't a clue. I think that's kept from us on purpose, so we're ready all the time." She thought about the little girl that he'd been watching when she'd been brutally murdered. "Sometimes it's as much a surprise to us as it is their families."

"I love you, Valyn. With all my heart." He kissed her on the mouth and she held his hand under the table. "Why don't we skip the movie and go straight home from here? I can almost hear the hot tub calling us."

"That's a wonderful idea."

They lingered over their pizza and enjoyed being together, neither of them talking about anything serious or about work. When they left, it was wonderful, like they'd been able to relax more than they had before.

~*~

Valyn wanted to take his time, wanted to make love to Jennifer in a way that would be good for them both. The last time, earlier this morning, he'd been too rushed to pay attention to what she might need. He wanted her to climax several times tonight instead of just the one. That was his mission tonight—to have his wife as limp as a wet noddle. That term he had learned today.

He undressed her, touching her skin when it was exposed to him. Kissing parts of her that he thought would be tender and make her shudder again. Valyn was discovering things about her while doing this.

She was ticklish. Kissing her at the base of her spine would send her into fits of giggles. Her underarms were also a place that would make her laugh. Jennifer's inner thigh seemed to call to him for a kiss, and there he could smell her scent, her need, like it was his own. But for now, he was going to avoid her there. He had a great deal left to explore.

The backs of her legs were especially taut, and he enjoyed rubbing them until they were soft and supple in his hands. Even the tops of her feet he found to be erotic. He loved her toes, the way she had them painted a bright red. The way her ankle turned when she was lifting it up for him to touch.

Valyn loved her bottom — the curve of the fine muscles, the two tiny indentations just at the top of the sway outward. There were small freckles there as well, places that got his full attention as he touched her.

"Valyn, I'm melting here. Please, I need to lie down, you've made me both tense and weak with your touches."

He remembered something that he'd heard, something that had gotten Riss his mate. Spreading out his wings, he took one of his feathers and rubbed it over her back, down her spine to her bottom.

Her scream of release had him biting hard on her bottom. It was that or scream with her. The most erotic feeling overwhelmed him when he'd put the feather to her skin, and he'd felt every stroke of it. Valyn decided to try her entire body with his part.

Standing up in front of her, he could see that she was indeed weak. Her eyes were glazed over, her knees trembling. Picking her up in his arms, he gently laid her on the bed and got down on his knees.

"This is a part of me. I can feel the same things you do when I stroke this over your body." He played with the feather over her nipple, and wasn't surprised to see the tip harden tightly, her breast swelling with need. His own felt ready, needy, and he leaned over and took the morsel into his mouth. The feather he brushed over her belly to her thighs. Then between her legs.

The climax exploded out of him. Her own cries of relief had him bending his head toward her. He'd never felt this way before, had never come this hard in his life. Looking at her when she begged him for more, he nearly told her that he couldn't, it was just too much, but then she kissed him.

The tangle of their tongues was delicious to him—the way her nipples barely touched his chest yet seemed to set him afire. Lifting his head enough to move to her throat, Valyn joined her on the bed, positioning himself between her creamy thighs.

Her heat seemed to pull at him. The need to enter her, to take her as she was begging him to do, had him slamming forward as hard as he could. It wasn't enough—the completion was close, but not there yet. Lifting her bottom up so he could take her deeper, he moved in and out of her quickly, needing to hit the finish line.

Everything stilled for a second—not a heartbeat could he heard. The clock on the wall seemed to pause, waiting for them to climax. And when they did, both of them crying out at the same time, he felt lifted up, dragged though something wonderous before he was dropping on top of her.

Valyn didn't move. He wasn't even sure that was possible after that. When Jennifer moved beneath him, he thought that he might be too heavy and boorishly, moaning and groaning the entire time, he rolled to his back.

Her giggle had him looking at her with one eye. Right now he didn't think that he had the strength to open the other one, if ever again. She was lying there, beautifully sated, her body red and somewhat bruised by his treatment of her. But even with that, he thought her the most gorgeous creature he'd ever seen.

"I can't move." He groaned that he couldn't either. "What on earth gave you the idea to touch me with your feather? That was mind blowing to say the least."

"Riss, he told me." She glanced at him with a cocked brow; he knew that to mean he'd better explain. "He didn't give me any details of what he'd done with it, but he mentioned that it would be fun. Did you think it was fun?"

"No, it was a killer." He grinned, thinking that sounded very good to him. "Next time warn me. I might need to fortify myself for another round like that."

They lay there, each, he supposed, lost in thought. When she rolled over to his side of the bed and put her head on his chest, he held her there, thinking this was a perfect ending to his day. When she spoke, he could barely hear what she was saying, but he wasn't sure that he was supposed to for some reason.

"It's a dream, this love of him. I'm going to wake up and this will be a good dream and there won't be a Prince Charming. There won't be a lovely castle. I'll just be living in my car, hoping to find work again." It broke his heart to hear her say those things.

He'd never celebrated Christmas, but he had seen plenty of them in his years of being a Protector. He was going to give her one. The best one she could ever have.

Slipping out from under her, he sat on the side of the bed and watched her sleep. It was dark now, the house was silent, so he dressed himself and made his way downstairs. He had no idea where to start on something like this, and went to find out what he could. Riss, like the rest of them, wasn't asleep, and he asked them all to join him.

"The date is passed, you know—the one that they celebrate it all. I don't suppose you want to wait until next year?" Valyn told Agon what he'd found out today. "Oh well, we really need to do this. Tonight, if we can."

"I don't know where we could find a tree and decorations." Tholan came into the study where they were all gathered and put out his hand. In it was the smallest decorated tree he'd ever seen. "It's beautiful, but I don't think I could get many gifts under that, do you?"

"Don't be silly. I was told that you just set it on the floor where you want it and it will do the rest. I've taken the liberty of wrapping some gifts for her myself. And the other females. A large meal is something that you should plan on as well." They were all in agreement. "To be honest with you about the tree, I've no idea other than I was told you only need to set it down. For all I know, it could be a spindly tree without any form or color on it."

Valyn couldn't decide where to put it. Riss suggested the bedroom, and Arryn thought the study was a good place. But Riss told him that he should place it in the entrance way, near the grand staircase. He said he'd seen that in a movie once.

They all went to the front hall and Valyn took the tiny tree. He set it on the floor and stepped back. Whatever was going to occur, he didn't want to be in the way. He might end up being decorated as well. When nothing happened, he looked at Tholan for advice.

"Oh, I forgot in my excitement to bring it to you. Valyn, you must breathe on it. Don't ask me why, but that was what the note said when I found the tree on my desk." Valyn asked him if he thought it was a joke. "I don't have a sense of humor; you of all people should know that."

Yes, they all did. He never got sarcastic banter, nor did he get jokes. After it was explained to him why something was funny or not, he still had trouble grasping the idea why anyone would do that to someone else.

Valyn went to the tree and blew his breath over it, nearly knocking it over when he did. Stepping back a second time, he knew this was a joke. It wasn't until the tree started to shake that he thought this was going to work. As the tree grew to a mammoth size that fit in the hallway, he watched as the rest of the house was decorated as well.

The staircase railing was wrapped in greenery. The candles in the window were surrounded by a beautiful wreath. Sparking lights were put up around doorways and overhead. Even the study that they had been in was beautiful. But the dining room was the best of all.

There was a second tree, much smaller than the one in the hall but no less decorated. There were lights galore in the room as they entered, and the table started to fill with food. Turkey, still steaming from the oven. Ham that was decorated as well, with pineapple and cherries. There were green beans, corn on the cob, as well as stacks of warm sliced bread. More was sprouting up every second, too much for him to see all at once.

Turning to Riss when he nudged him, he turned and found Jennifer in the hall staring up at the tree. "I know it's not the traditional holiday date, but we thought—"

She leapt into his arms before he could finish. With her kissing him all over his face, he held her tightly, so happy that she was.

"It's my very first tree. I've never put one up before

when I could, because who would see it but me. Oh Valyn, this is the best holiday I've ever seen." He told her that it was his first as well. "I love you for this. It's wonderful."

Before too long the wives showed up, dressed in bright green and red clothing. Even he got in on the fun and wore a striped shirt of the same colors, along with pointy shoes. For some reason, he thought them to be funny. He supposed they were; everyone was entertained making fun of him. And he didn't care. He was as happy as he'd ever been.

CHAPTER 6

Samuel made reservations at the bed and breakfast in the little town. The problem was, there wasn't anything they could rent out until the end of the month. It was only the fourth, but she told him that people came from all over to see the decorations. Even though the holiday had passed a week ago they still had visitors coming in, so the town left the decorations up longer. It took him a moment or two to remember what holiday she was talking about.

She said that she'd call him if there was a cancellation, but she said not to count on it. She'd been booked up since Christmas last year. When Betsy came into the room, he told her about it.

"That's preposterous. Why would anyone travel in this weather to see a bunch of lights and tinsel?" She didn't seem to require an answer, so he didn't voice one. Not that he knew what to tell her, but that was the way it was. "Oh, I found out about our other deadbeat, Ashley Knisley. She told me that she had no money to give to me—she just can't spare it. After you giving her that speech and all."

"Once we have this all settled with the Hale woman, we'll send a cop after her. Do you still have the number of that guy who has a uniform? I don't remember his name." She told him. "Oh yes, that's it. Brandon Williams. I'll call him next and have him go to her house and threaten her. That usually works quickly. Funny how they come up with the cash when a cop shows up, isn't it?"

"Do you think we should send him after the Hale woman? Maybe we won't have to do all this if he can get her to pay up." He was actually looking forward to going, but told her to go ahead. It couldn't hurt. "Good, I'll go and call him now." She left him there while she made the call.

Samuel never understood why she went to an entirely different part of the house to make calls. There was a perfectly good phone on the desk he was sitting at. Not to mention, there were about a dozen burner phones that she could have used too. So while she was doing her thing, he began looking up information about who this Slayer person might be.

He'd not gotten a first name, but the last was easy enough to search for. There were only two in the phone book, but when he called directory assistance, he found out there were actually three. That was the number that he'd called yesterday, and he was set to call there today. He'd gotten no call back from the woman, and nothing to indicate that she'd even gotten the message. Pulling the phone toward him, he called again.

The same cultured voice answered, and he told him who he was. Samuel was glad that he'd written down the name that he'd used, or he would have been stumbling around trying to remember.

"If you'd like to wait, sir, the lady of the house and Lord Slayer are here now. One moment, please." When the phone was taken off hold the man cleared his throat as if he was trying to stifle a laugh or something. "The lord of the house is going to take the call, sir. I will transfer you to the study now."

Woo hoo, he thought, *a study*. And what was all this crap about being Lord Slayer? The Internet search hadn't said anything about him being that. Just as the phone was answered, he was writing down to find out what he could about lords and ladies of the house.

"Mr. Cochran, this is Valyn Slayer. I'm to understand that you wish to speak to my wife? She's resting. Can I help you?" This was better than he'd thought. He'd just hit the man up right away for the cash. "Sir?"

He'd taken too long in basking over the good news and had to scramble to get back on track. When he looked down at his notes, he knew that none of them were going to be helpful and was disappointed in that.

"Yes, I'm still here. I've got a good many things going on today." Shit, that sounded lame. "Jennifer Hale, now Slayer I'm to understand, was court-ordered to pay back on a credit card that she abused. Since the last payment from her, we've not heard anything from her. And now we find out that she's moved as well as gotten married. This is quite a large sum of money we're trying to get back. I know you'll understand now why it's important that I speak to her."

"I see." That didn't really tell him much, so he waited. And waited. Finally the man spoke. "And this credit card that she supposedly abused, can you tell me which company it was given to her by? That way I can call them directly and see if I can make better arrangements."

"Oh no, we're handling this. The credit card company has us do all their collections. They don't have the manpower to chase after everyone that charges a large amount. We're just working for them." He asked again for the name of the company. "I'm not sure that I can give you that, sir. It's been mandated that she pay us — the company back, and she's not done that."

"Can you hold on for a moment?" Before he could tell the man that his time was more valuable than to wait while he got his thumb out of his ass, he'd pressed the button too quickly. "Becker Credit Union. I have it now."

He was dumbfounded on what to say next. How the hell did he get that? Then he remembered that Jennifer was there, and she would have told him. The man was speaking, and he missed a little of what he was saying. After asking him to repeat himself, the man laughed.

"I said, are you aware that there is no listing for Becker Credit Union? Not only that, but there doesn't seem to be any kind of registration for the name at all." Again, he was shocked and told the man he didn't know what he was talking about. "I'm sure you don't. Why don't you do this? You come here and collect the money that my wife is supposed to owe your company. I'll need a receipt, of course, when I pay you, but that will be easier and quicker than sending it through the mail system. That way you can take it off your books, and I won't have to be nickel and dimed about it. What do you say?"

"Well, that sounds good, but the local bed and breakfast doesn't have any openings until the end of the month. Also, just so we're clear on this, Miss Hale owes my company over fifty thousand dollars, and with penalties and interest it'll be more. Then we must add on the late charge and my having to come there to get it. Let me see what a good price — uhm, what the updated total would be."

He fuddled around until he could get himself under control. Samuel hated when people babbled, and here he was doing the same thing. He was also having a hard time keeping his story straight. That had never happened to him before. After taking several calming breaths and letting them out slowly, he felt as if he could talk to the man again.

"The additional charges will be three hundred and ten dollars." He thought that sounded less like he'd made it up and more like he had taken the time to add it up. "We'll need that additional money as well."

"Of course. And I'll have a talk with Mrs. Peach and see if she can get you into her place a little earlier. That way you won't have to put any more charges on the bill." Thanking him, he told him he'd look forward to hearing from him. "Yes, I'm sure that you will."

The man was very cryptic, he thought after hanging up. He had a feeling he'd missed something here and there in the conversation but felt he'd covered himself well. Writing down all the things that they'd talked about, he decided to wait until the end of the month anyway, and tack on a few more charges. No matter when she could work him in, it was going to be a conflict with something he had going on here.

Collecting the money all at one time was going to be nice too. The way they were getting it now, monthly payments coming in, didn't leave them very much to do anything with. Well, he supposed that someone else would think an income of twenty-five grand a month would be wonderful. But they had expensive tastes, and the love of good restaurants too. Rubbing his hands together, he thought about what he was going to do with all that extra cash coming in. Yes, this was wonderful.

After telling Betsy about what he and *Lord* Slayer had talked about, she sat down and zoned out again. He was a little perturbed that she wasn't as excited as he was about it. But then, she rarely got excited about anything. When she looked at him, he felt his cock shrink and his balls sort of cinch up to his body. It was painful to say the least.

"I'm going to go with you." He nodded. Actually, Samuel had thought she was anyway. "I'm going to talk to this girl about the way things are going to be from now on. I mean, her husband can pay us the amount, but we're going to find other ways to get more out of her."

"Do you think that's a good idea? I mean, he is willing to pay us over fifty grand, you know?" She nodded. "All right. That's the way we'll do it. Am I going to go along with you? I'd like to see this man, for the simple reason I think he was poking fun at me."

"Yes, of course you're going to be there. I'd have it no other way." He was glad for that. She could be a bit temperamental when she wanted to be. "I think we should buy us something special to wear. Perhaps you a fitted suit instead of your old dry cleaned one, and me a very business-like dress. That way we can impress them both with our presence and calmness during this sort of meeting."

Nodding, she left him again. He didn't have any idea why she thought they'd be uncalming, but he was ready to do whatever she said. Betsy was the one that had talked him into this job, and he wasn't going to naysay her this late in the game.

He made arrangements to go and have a suit fitted for him. It was a lot more complicated than he thought. Samuel thought that you simply went to the store, picked out a suit, and they'd hemmed it for you. Apparently he was to be measured and fitted with the suit that was to be designed just for him. That was a little much, but it was Betsy's idea and he would go along with it.

~*~

Valyn sat in the office alone for nearly two hours. He knew the time because the big clock in the hallway announced the time like a starting pistol in a big race. Every fifteen minutes, there was a ding. He thought it to be the most annoying sound when he was trying to think.

Going outside, he made his way to the other realm. It might not calm him, but perhaps if he could help for a few minutes, he might be better equipped to deal with things that were happening to Jenny and the credit card company.

Renie had come to him this morning and told him all she'd been able to find out about the company Becker Credit Union. It was a scam. She told him that she'd figured that out long before today, but she had information that he might be able to use to turn things in his favor. And when she left him with all she'd found, he'd been no closer to figuring out what to do than he had been before.

"Are you well?" He told Tholan that he had a great deal on his mind. "I see. And coming here, it helps you with this decision, if there is one?"

"No, not really. But the clock isn't dinging." Tholan looked confused. But instead of explaining, Valyn told him everything that he'd found out about the scam. "So, you see, I'm not sure what I'm to do. Have them arrested for this, or just get Jenny out of it so that she can be happy."

"Why don't you spend some time with them both? A couple of hours with each should do that, shouldn't it? I would imagine that if they are half the people you think them to be, then it would behoove you to know everything. I think that their watchers would enjoy such a break." Valyn said that would be most helpful. "All right. Let me go and find out who is assigned to them, and if they'd like to switch out for a few hours. You do remember that you cannot change the course they are on, only be there to guide them in the right direction."

"Yes, I remember. And thank you, Tholan." He nodded and left him for several moments. Valyn reached to Jenny to let her know what was going on. *So I don't know when I'll be home, but I think this will help us.*

Yes. And if this is a scam, and I have no doubt you're right about it, then perhaps we can help other people they've scammed as well. You don't believe any more than I do that I'm the only person they've done this to. He told her no, he didn't believe that either. *Good. You do what you need to there, and I'll be working until five. If you're not home by then, I'll know where you are. Have a good day, Valyn.*

You too, Jennifer. He could feel her happiness and knew that if Boss were to say anything about not paying her for the favor she was doing for him, Jennifer would do it for free.

He went to change places with the protector of Samuel Mercer. The man was being dressed. But then he figured out he was getting a new suit. As he was being measured, he wondered if he was planning to impress him and Jennifer, and had to laugh. Valyn wasn't impressed with what people wore. He was impressed by their mannerisms and the way they spoke.

"I have a very important meeting coming up soon. How long will this take?" The man told him a week. "All right. I'll just fob off that guy for a little longer. No big deal for the amount of money that we're going to get soon."

The tailor didn't take the bait, if that was what he was doing by dangling out there that they were getting money. The man who was measuring him for the suit had been a Protector until recently, and he didn't say a word. Valyn had to laugh when the man looked at him with a wink.

The Protectors that had been released a very long time ago were sent to this realm to do as much good as they could. Also, to rest and to take their life as they wanted to. Valyn hadn't understood why the group that he was with, his circle of friends, had always been told that their ending would be with death. And that once they decided that enough was enough for them, they would die a peaceful death.

But he'd found out recently that they were to be the Mystics, a power force that could and would train other Protectors about the world in general. How to blend in on their time off. Where the best place was to meet up with others like them. But most importantly, how to spend their money wisely. And most that he knew had quite a bit of it.

He watched Samuel interact with the tailor. The man was very shallow in the way he wanted to look—a black pinstriped, double breasted suit. The tailor, Dean his name was, hadn't once said anything other than what had to be asked about the suit. But when Samuel said he wanted that particular one for himself, Dean cocked his head and stared at the man.

"You cannot pull it off. You've a waistline that doesn't work well with a suit like that. You'd be better fitted if you were to wear a straight-line suit that would hide the bulge you have." Valyn watched Samuel's face turn bright red in his anger, but he only opened and closed his fist several times rather than speak right then. "I can do what you wish, Mr. Mercer, but you'll look like you've pulled your suit from one of the stores that also sells mints and beer."

"I believe you to be wrong about that. I'm as trim and fit as I've been since high school. I would like the double-breasted suit, and no more comments about how you think I have a bulge. I'll thank you for not doing things your way." That sounded pretty nice, and he had to admit, the man did have a big belly. But his next words were what he had expected from a man that would scam people for their hard-earned money. "You should be happy that someone like me comes to your rundown establishment. This place is nothing more than a fire hazard that is one lit cigar away from going up in flames. That might yet happen—you should be more careful."

He'd just threatened him. And not in any way that it could be mistaken for anything else. So, he watched Dean measure and pin the material in different places and thought that was the end of it. But Dean stood in front of Samuel when he was finished and gave him a threat of his own.

"You do know that you never insult a waitress before your food comes. She could spit in it or make the food come out wrong. The same with someone that is to make something for you. For instance, this suit." He helped him take the jacket off and laid it gently on the table before continuing. "You should be careful, Mr. Mercer. You have no idea what sort of friends I have in my corner. And we do not mess around."

There was complete silence during the rest of the visit. Since he was temporarily assigned to Samuel he had to follow him. But any kind of good will he'd had for him, if any, was blown out of the water with what he'd said to Dean. Yes, Dean had given as good as he got, but this man was also stealing from people, and that wasn't going to go over well when they next met in person.

The rest of the two hours was spent with him ordering shoes from the local store, going to have lunch by himself, as well as the rental of a limo. He wasn't impressed. Valyn had seen enough of these kinds of people, people that were only out for how they looked rather than how friendly they could be. Today had been an eye opener. And he couldn't wait to watch over the woman.

Going back to the station, he was briefed on a couple of things. Betsy was a little odd. She had done a great many drugs when she had been younger, and it had affected her mind somewhat. Her filter was gone in what she said as well. Also, she was dying of cancer, but didn't know it as yet.

When he was with her, the first thing he noticed about her was the strange way she was staring off in the distance. And as if she was waking, her thoughts just came out of her mouth. The poor waitress that had been waiting on her got a tongue lashing that was both cruel and loud.

Valyn watched her Protector talk to the waitress, sending her little bits of happiness. A way to deal with the pain of being treated that way. Valyn wanted to tell Betsy that it was unkind to do what she'd done, but he was there only to observe, not help. When she was served her meal, she did notice it wasn't the same waitress and laughed about it, talking to herself as if she was someone within ear shot of her meanness.

"I certainly taught her a lesson. I hope she's gone home crying. Stupid girl didn't even have the decency to bring me my hot rolls when I asked for them." Betsy looked around the room and no one was paying her any mind. "This is the dumbest town I've ever lived in. I have to tell you that."

"No, you do not." The restaurant manager came from the back room and stood by her table. Then when he sat down with her, Valyn moved closer. "I'm going to sit right here with you, and remind you every time you open your mouth that this is not a place where we tolerate being mean when you think you can."

"You don't talk to me that way." The manager, he had no idea what his name was, only leaned back in his seat. "Get away from me before I have you arrested for harassing me."

"Go ahead and call them. I'm sure that they'd be just as happy to take you away for disturbing the others in my restaurant, and being beyond mean to one of my staff. Now eat, then get out. I don't want you here again."

She stood up and doubled up her fists. The manager did the same. He was bigger than her—not just in height, but the man was muscled and fit. If there was going to be a showdown, Valyn was going to have to help Betsy. Not that he wanted to, but that was his job. So going against what he'd been told but seeing no other recourse than to talk to her, Valyn spoke in a whisper in her ear.

Move back. He's not worth going to jail for. Betsy shook herself, as if she was ready even against his advice. *You have a meeting in a few weeks. How will you get there if you are in jail or hurt?*

"You're just lucky that I have things to do or I'd be mopping the floor with your head. And that stupid waitress. If you think I'm paying this bill, you're as stupid as she is." She wiped her hand across the table and all the dishes and cutlery landed on the floor and splashed on the manager's pant legs. Then with a manic laugh, she left the restaurant with him in tow.

He'd learned a lot about these two. They would prey on the weaker like it was their only pleasure in life. Take what others had, even in the form of food and broken dishes. They lied and cheated whenever they could, even over little things. And he was going to take them both down.

Going back to where he'd left several hours before, Valyn sat down again, this time with Tholan and Michael. He told them what he'd witnessed and how he'd spoken to the woman to keep her from getting hurt.

"You did well, Valyn. Even though you could have steered her in the wrong direction, you helped her. I'm proud of you." Valyn wasn't used to such compliments for just doing his job, and thanked Michael for it. "Your wife, she is having a much better day today. Making friends and talking to people. She is someone that would have made a great Protector. Don't you think?"

"I do. But we're happy just where we are, thank you." They all three laughed and then Valyn took his leave.

As soon as he entered his home, he thought something had happened. The house was very quiet.

"Oh, there you are." He turned toward the study to find Jennifer there. She kissed him soundly and hugged him. *This*, he thought, *is what I've lived for my entire life.* "I might have overstepped my boundaries today. No one was mad, but I ordered a few planters to put in the dining room at the hospital. They brightened it up considerably."

"Why would anyone be upset about that?" She looked up at him. "Oh, I can see that I'm asking the wrong question. Just how many plants did you order?"

"Just a few more to go in the hallways on the way there. Also, someone is going to come in and fix the fountain that hasn't worked in several years. He's going to put koi in it because they're so entertaining." She told him the number of planters she had ordered. "You're not mad at me, are you? I'll pay you back for it all. It might take me awhile — I don't make anything for the work I'm doing."

"Why on earth would you think that I'd be mad at you for taking the time to spruce up the hospital? No, it's a lovely idea. When I had to be with someone that was close to passing, I often wondered why there was no greenery in the place. No cheer. I know that it's not always a place that would appreciate that sort of thing, but I think it's wonderful, and I cannot wait to see it."

"I'm so glad to hear that. Because if this goes well, they're going to come here and do our yardwork, as well as put in a few dozen flowers and plants when spring comes." With a quick kiss she left him there, only to pause and look over her shoulder toward him. "I'd like to also learn how to drive, if you have time."

He was still laughing when he made his way to the kitchen for dinner. They'd been eating in that room because the dining room was so formal, and they liked the company that was in the big warm room. Tomorrow he was going to find someone to teach her to drive. He might not be hurting so much all the time if someone showed her rather than him. She might get testy with him.

Chapter 7

Samuel had listened to the story about the incident in the restaurant twice now, and it didn't sound any better than it had before. When they made waves by bringing attention to themselves, bad things could happen. He was glad now that they were going on this little jaunt. It might be good for people to have cooler heads. At least he hoped so.

The limo that he'd ordered to pick them up was a little late. But he didn't mind right now because they were going to be fifty thousand dollars richer. And since it was the end of the month, in just a few days they'd have all the payments coming in. It was a good day for him.

"What are you smiling about?" He told her as they sat in the dining room of their rental. "You looked like you've something or someone up your bung. Who is he? Anyone I know?"

He glanced around to see if anyone was listening. He wished now that he'd not told her that he was a homosexual while he was drunk one night. She'd been hanging that over him whenever she got the opportunity ever since. There was something seriously wrong with Betsy. And it had all started when she'd come back from getting measured for her business dress.

"You have to keep your voice down." She glared, and he had a moment of fear. "We're treading on thin ice here, Betsy, and if we get into any more trouble, we might not make it to this meeting at all. Please, it's going to be a big payoff, and I don't know about you, but I'd like a nice vacation."

She stilled, and he waited while looking around to see if the staff might have heard her. The house they were renting had come with servants, and that had suited them both just fine as they neither one did any house work.

"All right, but don't think you've won this round, David. I know where you live." He asked her who David was and she waved him off. "Never you mind. I've got him under control no matter what he tells you."

She was getting stranger and stranger every day. But this, this last day had been especially weird. When he asked her again what had happened when she'd been out, she looked at him as if she didn't know him.

"I had lunch in the diner, as I told you about. The proprietor of the place, he kicked me out because one of his waitstaff was whiney and insulted by what I said to her." He swallowed hard before asking her what the girl had done. "She said that she'd bring me coffee and I got it, but there wasn't any cream on the table. And then she brings me those little packets of stale milk. You know that's not fit to drink. So, when I tried to train her on what she'd done wrong and how to do it better, she cried. I just can't stand when someone cries when I'm speaking to them."

"Yes, yes, I know that about you. Did you perhaps tell her how she was doing it wrong in a calm way? Or were you too upset to do that?" She said that she'd yelled at her, but the girl had been wrong. "All right then. It's done, and we're on our way when the limo arrives. It should be here very soon. I would imagine it's the traffic."

"What time did you order it to be here? Samuel, you know that you have to give an extra hour on things like this. People are forever taking advantage of people."

He said nothing more as the limo pulled up in front of the house just as she told him that. Getting the luggage into the car was easy. The driver told them that he was sorry, but there was an accident on the highway and he was thinking that they should take the round route, so as not to lose time. Samuel agreed. Anything to get the money. The driver laid his suit along with Betsy's on top of the luggage, so they wouldn't get mussed. As they were getting themselves situated, he looked around. This was his first limo ride, and he was going to enjoy it.

Of course, Betsy complained the entire drive. It wasn't a long one, only three hours, but with her lambasting him about every little thing, it seemed twice as long. She complained about how the seats were not leather and heated for her. Then she was upset that they didn't have any beer in the small fridge, but wine and small containers of cookies.

"I don't know why they think that this baby food is

going to be satisfying to us. You should have told them that we were grownups and that we eat grownup food." He said that he'd remember that for the next time. "No, you won't. I'll take care to order it from now on. I think that I should start having more say in the business."

"You own half of it, Betsy. What more do you want from it?" She told him that she wanted eighty percent. "That's quite different than we discussed when we got together. I mean, you're only leaving me with twenty percent. And that's not fair."

"I don't care if it's fair or not. I'm the one that has to keep people in line when we need something. Also, there is the little matter of this lord, or whatever he is. You two are in cohorts, fucking each other like nasty men do." He asked her where on earth that had come from. "I don't know. I'm not sure."

She laid her head back on the seat and said nothing more for the rest of the ride. Betsy being this quiet worried him, and he didn't know why. When they were finally at the bed and breakfast, he helped her out of the car and into the establishment. All he could see was the entrance hall, and he was impressed. After giving the famous Mrs. Peach their names, she took them right up to their rooms and helped him help Betsy to lie down.

"Are you going to be all right here by yourself?" Betsy waved him off and told him to go away. "All right. But I'm going down to dinner now. If you feel better before I get back, come join me."

Again she waved him off with a loud "Fuck off." He smiled then. Betsy was going to be fine now, he knew it.

100

And all this talk about her taking most of the business, it was her not feeling well.

He was seated in the dining room when a cordless phone was brought to him, and was told it was Lord Slayer.

"Are you really a lord?" Samuel didn't mean for that to slip out, and now that it was out there, he had to fix this. "I just wanted to know for my records."

Why was he so lame sounding around this man? There was something about him that Samuel didn't like, and he'd not even met him yet. When the man cleared his throat and laughed a little, Samuel took offense. But then, he was forever taking offense to something someone said to him when he was embarrassed. Letting out two long breaths, he waited for the man to answer.

"Yes, I'm to understand that you're in town. Mrs. Peach has gone to a great deal of trouble for you, so I do hope that you'll take care of her when you leave. She and her staff have been working hard for this visit." He didn't have any idea what that meant and assumed he planned to pay the bill. He wasn't like his wife, he wanted to point out; he did pay what he owed. "I have cleared my calendar for tomorrow for lunch. I'm hoping to get this cleared up then, and not have this worrying Jennifer again."

"Yes, I understand. Does she know that you're going to pay me the money?" He said that he didn't keep secrets from his wife or anyone else. "I see. A truthful man, then?"

"I am. And will be for a very long time. The limo will be there to pick the two of you up around eleven thirty. And then it will bring you to my home." Samuel had hoped that the meeting would be there at the hotel, on his ground so

101

to speak, but the man was going to make sure he was paid, so he'd go along with him for now. "After the meeting, I'll go about my business and you will yours. I don't want you bothering nor harassing my wife or anyone in this family again. Do I make myself clear?"

He had a tone. That was all Samuel could think about was the man had a tone, like he was really pissed off at him for daring to ask for money. Well, it was his, and he had worked hard so that she would make him rich. That was clear as rain to him. but the man obviously didn't understand the rules of the game. Well, tomorrow he'd learn that Samuel Mercer and Betsy Whitaker were not to be messed with.

He had until noon tomorrow to get prepared. Samuel had thought that he was until the phone call. Now he wanted his answers and questions to be perfect. Before he even sat down, he had three drafts of questions to ask in his mind. He had yet to get to the statements he was going to make.

This man had made him feel like he wasn't up to snuff. As if he was less than him. Samuel was better than him, and more than likely had a good deal more money. He was glad now that Betsy had said to get a good suit. It made him feel powerful.

Ordering a small salad and half of a roast beef sandwich, he looked around at the others that were staying here. For the most part they were younger couples, and a few children. And all here to look at some lights that had been on every single house he'd passed on the way here.

"People are just stupid."

The salad was sat in front of him just as he said that. When the waitress asked him what he'd said, he only waved her off. He had to be careful here. Talking to himself would get him labeled as a goofball.

Eating the salad even as his belly rumbled for something more, he wondered what this man looked like. For that matter, why he had married so beneath him. Not that he was a snob or anything, but Jennifer was down on her luck, owed thousands of dollars out, and hadn't had even a decent suit when she'd been brought before the courts. She'd worn a pair of torn, yet clean, jeans and an oversized T-shirt.

Samuel could not wait until tomorrow. He was going to have this man eating out of his hand, he'd be so impressed with him.

When his sandwich was brought to him, he didn't even bother with looking at it before taking a nice bite of it. The burn of horseradish took his breath away, and as he tried his best to get the burning sensation to stop, he was inhaling the nasty stuff and that was making his eyes water. What the hell? Who put horseradish on a roast beef sandwich?

The trouble was, he couldn't yell at anyone. His throat was scorched bloody, he just knew it, and his eyes were so full of tears, he couldn't see well enough to see who to talk to anyway. Leaving the dining area, he made his way to his room and put his head under the faucet in the tub. The water felt glorious until it turned molten hot and he was hotter than before.

Christ, what happened to him having a good day? It

was down the tubes in just one bite of a stupid sandwich. He laid down on his bed and tried not to think of the burning. As he closed his eyes and tried to breathe through the pain, he thought of tomorrow.

"Tomorrow, I'll show them all."

He would too. Samuel had worked hard on this, and no one was going to take it from him this late in the game.

~*~

"I've found at least ten more people that they've pulled this scam on. Two of them have filed bankruptcy, and three of them have had to borrow money from the bank to pay them off when a cop came to their home demanding that they either pay up or he was going to run them in." Valyn asked Renie how much she thought they had netted from this. "Over the five years they've been doing this? I'd say more than a million dollars. Quite a racket they have going here. And before you ask me, I don't know who else is involved in this. I know one man—I'm trying to find his name."

"So Jennifer isn't the first." She told him that she wasn't the last either. "Why has no one found this out before now? I mean, don't they have to report that much income to the government? At least that's the way I'm to understand it."

"They demand cash—or in the case of Jenny, they want money orders. No way to track those if they cash them out. I mean, they can be traced, but no one takes the time to do that. I mean, why would they? They're just money orders made out to cash."

Valyn was trying to wrap his head around someone cheating and lying to people. For what? A bit of money?

He knew that this was a great deal of money; Kala was teaching them all the value of each denomination. But why did they need so much they'd steal it?

He looked at Renie when she said his name. "I don't understand." She nodded as if she knew what he was struggling with. "This is not the way to treat people. Especially those that have done nothing to them."

"I'm sorry to say that it goes on more than I'd like to think as well. As I was digging through this mess, I found where one person committed suicide rather than face her family after they were able to bail her out at a great cost to them. No one will believe these people when they say that they've nothing to do with this card or any of the companies that are involved." He asked her how many. "Ten that I can find so far. They switch out the name of the place every few people. That way they don't get much in the way of feedback. And when someone calls them at the beginning of their scam, they simply don't answer the phone. People get frustrated when they can't talk to anyone. And all they have is a P.O. Box somewhere."

He read over the information that she'd given him before leaving. Valyn tried very hard to not think about how many people they had hurt, and concentrated on just getting his facts straight. This was going to be a major take down, as Jennifer had called it, and he wanted to not stumble with the information.

Dusty entered his office just as he was putting things back in the folder to take a small break. "I found their banking account. It was fairly easy once I got with Jenny. She had a receipt that was given to her when she paid them the first time with a check. There is a bank stamp on the bank. After that, it was easy to find with their names on it." He asked her why that was important. "Because, my dear brother-in-law, I got the money out of it."

"That's cheating as much as them taking from Jennifer, isn't it?" She told him that the money would be used for good. "And what sort of goodness do you have in mind? I could use a bit of good news."

"I've put the money in a different account, one that only has a name on it and nothing else. However, I don't think these people are smart enough to figure out how to trace their funds. Anyway, once this is finished and they're both in jail, we can pay back some of the people who have nearly lost everything. I think there might be enough to pay at least a portion of what they were scammed out of." He asked her how much was in the account. "A little less than a million dollars. I've spoken to Galin, and we're going to put in enough so that everyone is paid back. At least those that we can find."

"You can add my name to that as well. I feel bad for these people." She said that she did too. "I have that meeting in the afternoon with them. I have called the Federal Bureau and was told that they'd be here as well, hidden away until I can get them backed into a corner. I don't really know what that means, but I'm going to wing it."

She laughed with him. "I have an idea. You might like this. How about I have the three people brought here that aren't that far away? That way they can finally face their enemies, so to speak. Not at first—just like the FBI, after you've backed them into a corner." Valyn liked that idea.

"Jenny said that she was going to be here too. I like that. This will be closure for a lot of people."

Jennifer had gone to work that morning even though it was supposed to be her day off. The people at the hospital were calming to her, and she needed that for a little while. She'd been so good at what she was doing that she had branched out to the local nursing home one day a week as well. Boss said she was helping a great many people in her kindness and willingness to listen.

"She's been very down of late. I'm not sure why." Dusty told him that she was worried. "I have her. I would never allow these people to harm her."

"No, you wouldn't. But doesn't mean that she won't be hurt. The heart is a tender thing, you know that." He did. It had been pointed out to him that there were different kinds of hurts. Mental, physical, as well as verbal. "And if I were you, I'd do what Galin does for me when I'm feeling overwhelmed. He takes me out to dinner, lavishes all kinds of gifts on me, and then he takes me soaring in the sky at night. The dinner and gifts pale considerably when I get to be free of everything but him and me up as high as I'd like to go."

He thought about that long after Dusty left to do some calling. Valyn knew that she'd not like gifts on the lavish side. She was simpler than that, a woman who would enjoy a homecooked meal as opposed to one that had been made in a restaurant. And while she enjoyed flowers of all kinds, she much preferred plants that she could grow and see bloom for her. But taking her on a flight, that would be something that they both could enjoy, he thought. He made his way to the kitchen to ask the cook about a couple of things

It was going to be perfect, he thought. When she came home tonight, tired and ready for dinner, he'd take her away. As he made plans to have a picnic dinner made up for the two of them, he thought of the thousands of trees that were just outside his window at his first home. Going there, Valyn picked out two of them to plant, as well as a few flowers that he thought she might enjoy.

He was just planting the flowers when Michael came to him. "This is a splendid idea, Valyn. She will be most happy that you've taken the time to do this for her." Valyn knew that wasn't the real reason he'd come to see him, and waited for it. "You will make her very happy. Yes, you will."

"What's happened? I know you well enough, my friend, to know when you are stalling. You repeat yourself, mumble when you should be talking, and you will not look me in the eye. What has brought you here?" Michael glanced at him but turned away without speaking. "Michael, will I need to call the others here to beat it out of you?"

"You jest." Valyn only stared at him. "Nay, you do not. I have come with some news that I'm not sure your mate will be happy with. Her mother is coming here. She has not been a part of her life for a great many years, and she saw in the newspapers that Jennifer has wed someone of wealth. Her name is Elizabeth Hale. She is going to be bad news, I think."

"You think, or you know this?" Michael said that it could go either way. "I see. And when is this person going to arrive? I'm sure that you know when."

"In a week. You have plenty of time to let Jennifer know." Valyn asked him why he had to tell Jennifer. "Because as much as I love her, she has gotten stronger in her ability to tell a person off. I believe she's been hanging around the others too much. She is no longer the sweet person that I first saw, but this person that.... Well, she's not the same as she was before, that's all."

Valyn laughed. It was comical to him to see this person, of all the men he knew, afraid of a slip of a woman. He decided to have some fun with him and told him that it was his responsibility to tell her. Of course that made him sputter and complain. In the end, after laughing hard for about ten minutes, he told Michael that he would tell her.

"But you might be called upon to answer questions about her. If I were you, I'd be prepared. As you said, she's not been in her life, nor a positive role model, for some time, and she will need answers." Michael said that he'd take care that he knew more than he did now. Having that settled, Michael gave him a handful of seeds that he pulled from his pocket.

"They are a rare breed, these plants. Some of them have not been seen by humans for a long time. I would keep them in a safe place or you will be overrun with people wanting to have a bit of them." Valyn said that he would make sure, then asked him what sort of sunlight they'd need. "You, that's all. You with your magic should stand by them at least once a week. Your radiance will be more than enough to make them blossom year after year for your mate."

Touching each of the dozen or so seeds, he knew what they were. He looked up at Michael when he got to the kadupul flower, a rare flower indeed. He told him that was a gift from him. There were also ghost orchids and a jade vine, one of Valyn's favorite flowers. Jennifer would love that they were her own special flowers, and he was going to make sure that he took care that they had what they needed to grow for her.

After planting them as he was told, he stood before the seeds in the earth and spread his wings. With his magic beating down on the soil that cradled them, he could see the small seedlings sprout from the ground. It would be a lovely spot not long from now, and he decided to make the place somewhere that Jennifer could go when she needed some time alone.

Valyn worked through most of the afternoon, and was satisfied that she'd enjoy his plans for her and love the pretty little seedlings that were growing in the area he'd picked out for them.

CHAPTER 8

Jenny was exhausted and hungry. All she wanted to do was to eat then go up and take a long hot bath. After that, she was going to go to bed. It had been a very stressful day for her. She'd been present when a child had died, by the hand of someone that was to keep him safe.

Having a long conversation with his Protector, she was no less angry about it. Not about the death, but with the story that he told her about the boy's fate and what he had been going through since he'd been born.

"They were unkind to everyone, and when someone would dare question their actions, they would take it out on the boy." She asked him if they were his parents, and had they paid for their crime against him. "Yes, they are both in jail. Their hearing has yet to happen. But they will serve a great many years for this. The last time he'd been at his home, they had beaten him severely and he sustained trauma to his brain. There was nothing else that could be done for him. I spoke to him every day, telling him what he would someday see when he passed from this world to someplace better."

"And he died today, while I was in the room with him." The Protector—he couldn't tell her his name for a reason that she didn't understand—told her that when she spoke to him, it was the kindness in her voice that had him feeling it was time. "But could they have helped him here? Operated or something on him so that he could have a better life?"

"Nay, they could not. There was much too much damage done to his head. There was very little left of the little boy he'd been." Jenny said that was so sad. "It is. Not the first child that has had this happen to him. Nor, sadly, will it be the last. Children are easy prey for those type of people. They have no one to turn to because the people who should be caring for them are their tormentors. And their trust levels are very low because of that."

She had gone on with the rest of her day, crying in a dark corner when she was able. Not for the fact that he had passed, but that he'd been put in that situation in the first place. As she was putting her things away in the locker that she'd been given, Boss appeared.

"I don't want to talk to you right now. Not just you, but anyone. I've had my heart hurt, and I just can't deal." He nodded, and when she sat down on the bench in the large room, he did as well. "Why couldn't he tell me his name? The Protector, he told me that he couldn't tell me his name."

"He has never chosen one." She asked him how that was possible. "When the Protectors are created, they are grown adults. They are given the chance to choose any name that they wish. When he was created, a long time ago, he said that there were just too many people that he admired, and he would give me his name at a later date. He has yet to pick."

"Thank you. I won't be so irate the next time someone says that to me. I thought it was a club secret or something." His laughter made her smile. "Spill it. You're here for a reason, and with the day I've had, just tell me so I can deal with it tomorrow."

"Can't a man just come to see a pretty woman?" She said that a normal man could, but not him. "Ah, my dear, you wound me deeply."

"Stop stalling. Is it really bad?" He shook his head. "Then what is it? I really would like to have some good news right now."

"I'm afraid that I don't have any for you right at the moment." She felt her heart race, afraid of the news. "Your mother is coming to you."

"I take it she's found out that I have married into money, and is coming here with some sad sob story that will make me give her a lot. Then what? She tries to drain us dry? She's done this to me before, you know." He said that he did. "Then what makes this time so different? I won't give her anything this time either. She abandoned me a long time ago, and that was the end of our relationship."

He said nothing, and she was afraid that he thought she was wrong. She didn't want to disappoint him. But before she could even begin to explain to him what she'd done to her all her childhood, Boss spoke.

"I'm so very sorry." She asked him if he was sorry for her not wanting to see her mother. "Nay, I am sorry that it has come to this with her. She has no one to blame but herself in this. And no matter the amount of times she was encouraged to treat you better, she did nothing. But she will come and not understand why you have discarded her from your life. I hope that you are brave enough to tell her why."

She thought of what he said a lot on her way home. Was she brave enough? Probably not. Jenny had been a wimp all her life where it concerned her mother. And she thought that the reason was, in the back of her mind she had thought—no, hoped—that she would someday be the mother that she needed. But never, in all the times that they'd spoken, was there any declaration of love or even her being sorry for her actions. So, she thought again, was she brave enough to stand up to her mom? Jenny supposed that would depend on what she said to her.

There wasn't a sound in the house when she opened the door. It was an eerie kind of quiet, like the house was waiting for someone to turn it on. She knew that was silly, but she couldn't think of anything else. Then she saw the note on the front hall table.

My darling Jennifer. Meet me in the back yard and bring a jacket with you. I shall keep you warm. Love you always, Valyn.

Dropping her purse and work bag on the table, she made her way through the house to the back yard. There was no one there, and she thought she might have misread where to go. Then Valyn landed on the soft snow with his wings spread out behind him. He was the most beautiful

114

being she'd ever known.

"Come here. I have a nice surprise for you. I know you had a bad day, so I'm hoping this will make it better."

She moved across the deck slowly so as not to fall. But before she was to the steps, Valyn scooped her up in his arms and soared to the sky.

The sights were breathtaking from this view. She could see the tops of homes, the restaurant that she had worked in at one time. There were children out in the weather, dragging their colorful sleds behind them as they climbed the big hill.

Tops of trees were stunning against the backlighting of snow. Tiny looking cars were driving along the roads too. She could see lights still hung up on some homes, and they were like a twinkling beacon in the darkening sky. With the wind blowing gently over her face, it washed away her mood and replaced it with a much better outlook on life. Then Valyn took them to a mountain top and set her on her feet.

"How did that work with your mood?" She kissed him rather than tell him. She conveyed as best she could how magical the night had been for her. "I love that answer. But the surprise doesn't end there. Come on, I have a fire for you to get warm by."

There wasn't just a fire going, with the small bits of wood flames lighting up the sky. He had spread out a blanket on the ground and a large picnic basket in the middle of it. She went to sit on the blanket while he emptied the contents of the basket between them.

"Boss said that he told you about your mom." She

told him that she didn't want to talk about anything but the night. "All right. We can do that. I love the way your laughter seemed to come from someplace deep within your body. I've never heard such a delightful sound as that."

"You keep that up and you might get lucky, big boy." She ate some of the crackers and cheese that he had. When he handed her a glass of juice, she smiled at the taste—it was cherry. "You take such magnificent care of me. I don't know what I would have done had you not come around to loving me."

"I was a fool for pushing you away." She didn't disagree with him and he laughed. "I can see I still have a bit to make up for, don't I?"

"No. You've more than made up for your bad manners." He laughed again as he handed her a plate of food piled with delights such as cold fried chicken, potato salad, and macaroni salad. "You're trying to fatten me up for something, aren't you?"

"Just to show you how much I love you. And giving you some extra energy for later." They ate their meal while enjoying the beautiful night. "We will have to do this when it's warmer. The trees will be budding soon, and that is a sight you shouldn't miss."

"Warmer would be nice." She was warm, really. The fire next to them was giving off a great deal of heat. "I needed this today. More than you could know."

She told him of the little boy and what she'd learned from his death. He didn't say anything at first, and Jenny worried if talking about it would bring up hurtful memories for him. When she told him she was sorry, he told her that wasn't what he'd been thinking about at all.

"I was wondering about children. I cannot father any, sadly, but I would like to raise some children with you. That is if you'd like to as well." She wasn't really sure about that. She told him that she knew very little about them. "I have a good deal of experience watching people with children. I know when to change diapers, that there are different cries depending on what they wish. Also, I have noticed that when they're walking, things must be put up higher, so they cannot get into it."

"I would love to have a couple of kids running around here. I don't care if they're infants or older children that might need someone to be there for them. A place to come to when the world is too much for them." He told her that they'd never leave home then. "And that's all right too, I think. How do we start this process? I'm sure that it's not as easy as just saying we want to adopt children."

"No, but we have a great many of our kind in places where they would come to know where a child is being born. And which children will be alone in the world because of one thing or another." She nodded. thinking of the little boy from today. "And children, as you said, need a place they can come to when the world is too much."

"You mean like when they're taken from their parents for some reason." He told her that was what he meant. "They'll be hurt in some way, these children that would come to us. What will I do when they're taken away again? I love every child that I come in contact with. That'll be the hardest thing I have to do."

"Me as well. And there have been times when the

child just cannot go back to their family. We would help care for him or her until someone else comes forward and claims them too." She asked him if he had a child like that in mind. "No. But I only need to ask Tholan if he hears of something like that, to let us know. The paperwork for us will be handled by the right people as well."

"All right. Let's do it. I'm not sure how I'll make this work with my job, but I want to more than anything." He sat up and kissed her. "Just be warned that you're changing every poopie diaper there is."

They were both still laughing and talking about it when they made their way home. She was glad for the break in this crazy life, and was more than grateful for the man who had done it for her. Now back to reality and what was coming up tomorrow.

~*~

The meeting was about half an hour from happening. Jenny was afraid, she'd be glad to admit that, but more than that, she was pissed off. Every time she thought of what these people had done to her and others, she wanted to hunt them down and beat the snot out of them. She took some comfort in the fact that they were going to jail for a very long time.

"You'd look very pretty if not for the scowl you have on your face at the moment." She laughed when the man sitting next to her spoke. "There, that's much better. You must be Jennifer Slayer. I've heard a great deal about you. You cannot know how much it means to me to have this taken care of. My daughter lost everything when this started. And now that she's gone, I want this settled more than ever."

She had heard that someone had killed themselves over this mess, and that made her twice as mad. These people had so much to answer for. At least at the end of this meeting, everyone was going to get some portion of their money back. Not all — there were simply too many that hadn't come forward yet. And since they had no idea how many that might be, they were holding the rest in a trust to pay them. If nothing more came up, then the rest of it would be paid to those who had gotten their money already.

When Samuel and Betsy came into the room, they were shown to the seats right in front of Valyn's desk. She knew this because all of the rest of the people that would get to confront them with her were in another part of the house, watching the monitor that had been set up for the FBI. They were most interested in their confession. She was as well.

"My goodness. This is a grand house. Must have put you back a lot of money." Valyn said nothing to Samuel's comment. "Well, I suppose you want to get this over with. I have an accounting of all the money that she's paid us, as well as how much more she owes. As you can see, she made very few payments before she just stopped."

"And these other charges that you have here. What exactly are they for? You never said that it would be this much when I spoke to you the other day. You claimed that it would be three hundred and ten dollars." Samuel said that they were late fees, hotel fees for coming here. A car had to be used, as well as the time and energy that they'd wasted in coming here. "Yes, I do agree with you as to it being a colossal waste of time. And this fee here, the one that is for six thousand dollars. I don't see an explanation of what that is for."

"That is the cost of what my partner had to spend on finding where the young lady was. You can imagine that sort of information isn't easy to find." Again, Valyn didn't comment. "I've noticed that you have a nice view of the outdoors from here. That's what Betsy and I want for ourselves someday."

"Do you now? Well, I wish you luck with that. I'm thinking that it's going to be a long way off before you get around to that." Samuel asked him what he meant. "This house and the grounds cost a great deal more than you currently have in your checking account. And you hold no securities or any kind of other land. I don't think this house is in the cards for you. But I would like to speak to you —"

"You had no right to investigate us. None at all. We came here in good faith, to be paid the money that is owed to us." Valyn asked if Jennifer owed him or the company. "The company. That's what I said. And she will pay even if we have to contact the local police department to have her arrested."

Benny walked in eating a piece of cake. He had been asked to just come into the room, but with the cake in his hand, he looked like he'd been caught with his hand in the cookie jar. Valyn introduced them to the detective.

"Valyn, this cake is delicious. You'll have to give me the recipe, so I can have Lily make it some night." Valyn nodded and then told them who Benny was. "I was here when he said that you were coming. I didn't think you'd mind if I sat in on this with you. Do you?"

Samuel was blustering. So when Betsy spoke, it was as if they were Jekyll and Hyde between the two of them. Jenny had to cover her mouth when Betsy stood up near Valyn's desk and then he stood up too. She seemed to not be aware or didn't care that Valyn was much larger than she was.

"Just write the fucking check so we can get out of here. We've wasted enough time on that little shit to last two lifetimes." She slammed her hands on the desk as she continued. "You ever cross our paths again and I will make you regret it for the rest of your life. And that would include that cheat."

"Cheat? It's funny that you should mention that. I have some paperwork here that says that you two are cheats. You've taken a great deal of money from people that didn't do anything to you other than to be targeted in your sick game. Some people have lost a great deal in this. Do you have anything to say about it?"

"Yes, I do. Fuck them. If they want to scam people like us, then they're going to have to get up very early to do so. We've worked on this for years, and now that we have it perfected, you come along and sour the pot." Betsy pulled out a gun and pointed it at Valyn. "Now, you're going to pull out your fucking checkbook and write it out for the full amount. Then, after we're gone, you'd better look forward to us calling on you again. You never know what's going to happen to your darling wife."

"Did you just threaten him?" Benny looked at Valyn, then at Betsy again. Samuel was trying his best to get her to shut up and go with him. "You did. You just threatened a man in front of a cop. What the hell is wrong with you?"

"Nothing, and shut your trap. I'm going to take care of you too. You don't seem to be writing a check there, boy. Do I have to prove to you just how serious I am?" The gun went off and Benny fell off the desk. Jenny knew in her mind that he wasn't dead, but her heart said to run and get to him. She watched as Valyn pulled out a large notebook from the top drawer. "You might as well add another zero or two onto that amount. And for no other reason than I told you to."

"This isn't my checkbook. It's a list of names of the people that we know of that you've scammed. Besides my wife."

As he read off the names of the people that had been called upon to bear witness to these people being taken down, Samuel was sitting on the floor sobbing.

"This isn't what I practiced. You were supposed to be impressed at how I was dressed. And you were to pay attention to my words. You've done none of those things. You've upset Betsy." Valyn continued to read the names as Samuel spoke from his position on the floor. The gun going off again startled Jenny as she made her way into the large room. The shattered glass behind Valyn was a relief. She'd not shot him. "There you are. You're the cause of all this. Had you just paid like I told you to, none of this would be happening."

"No, you're right about that. You would have gone on using that credit card scam on a lot more people, wouldn't you have?" He told her that it was a perfect plan and that he was going to continue using it until he couldn't. "Really? I do believe that your days are over, Samuel. There is nothing now to keep you out of jail."

The police and the FBI came into the room with them all. They were armed and wearing flak jackets too. When they began shouting at Betsy to drop the gun, Samuel started screaming at Jenny again. This wasn't her fault.

They were arrested for a long laundry list of deeds they had committed. Betsy had finally dropped the gun, but she was no less abusive to the men who cuffed her. Samuel was still going on about his suit, and something about the people who were in the room. She didn't know what he was saying, so couldn't say if it was nasty or not.

"Are you all right?" She nodded at Benny when he was helped to stand up. The blood on his shirt scared her a little. "I'm fine. Like you, I'm an immortal. I can be hurt, which saves me a great deal of trouble when I'm shot like this, but I won't die."

Just as they were being taken out to the van that had come to get them, Betsy took off running. It was funny to see this woman in heels and a lovely skirt and blouse running in the rocks and snow. She was taken down by one of the police that was there for support. But she bumped her head bad enough to bleed, so they took her to the hospital.

This was the oddest arrest that she'd ever seen. Of course, she hadn't seen that many, but it was odd. As the house was emptied of the people there getting their checks, she sat in the corner of the room and thought about her life since meeting the Protectors and the Mystics.

It hadn't been boring, that was for sure. And she had

everything that she'd ever dreamed of with Valyn. Someone to love her, unconditionally, for the rest of her life. And now they were talking about children and helping others out. She smiled at him when he came around the corner toward her.

"Are you all right?" She said that she was perfect. "Well, I'm glad that you finally figured that out. Betsy is headed to the hospital, as you know. Boss wants us to go there and see that she gets cared for. I said that we would."

As she was pulling on her coat, she remembered what she'd been told about Betsy. She wondered if this was the time that they found out. Not having any idea what sort of cancer she might have, she worried all the way there.

They met up with the doctor not long after they arrived. "I'm afraid that I have bad news for you, Valyn. I'm telling you this because you were nice enough to come here to check on her." She held tightly onto Valyn's hand and waited for the doctor to explain. "While doing a routine imaging of her head, to rule out any damage that might have been caused by the bump, we found a tumor sitting atop her brain. It's been there long enough that its sort of taken over and dug its disease deep within her. There is no hope of us operating on it now. It's too massive."

"What happens to her now? Will she go to jail?" The doctor, another person married to a Protector, told her no, she was beyond that now. "What do you mean, beyond what?"

"Having a normal life. As soon as she was wheeled out of the imaging room, she had a stroke. And it has incapacitated her to the point where she is getting help to

124

breathe now. If we were to take her off the ventilator, I'm afraid that she'd simply not exist any longer. Someone is telling Mr. Mercer now. And asking if she has any family that we can call. I'm sorry."

They went to see her in the room she was in. Betsy was hooked up to all kinds of equipment, and all of it looked like it wasn't getting much of a reading. Jenny went to stand by her bed and took her hand into hers.

"I know that you know what's going on. I'm sorry for this. And the fact that you're not going to be able to move around and be yourself any longer. I really am sorry for that. None of us meant for this to happen to you." Valyn came to stand behind her, holding her as she continued. "There is a very nice woman here to take you beyond this life. She's been watching over you since you took your first breath. And she will be here when you take your last. I don't think you could be in better hands than that."

They left after that. The day was over, but there was still one more thing she had to deal with. And at this point, she was going to be able to say to her mom, fuck off. Jenny knew that she'd feel better when it was done too.

"I'd like for you to put it out that we want a child to raise. I'm ready to help someone to the right path. All right?" Valyn told her that he loved her. "And I love you. We'll make awesome parents."

"Yes, we will."

CHAPTER 9

"I have a child for you. Actually two of them, if you should want them together. They are brothers, and have been neglected for a very long while." Valyn asked Tholan how old they were. "The oldest is Connor Bass at seven. The younger one is Davy Bass—I believe it's short for David—and he is four. He's the most traumatized. They have been living in an abandoned house for the last few weeks. They left the home they shared with their father when the death smell was too much for them."

Valyn held onto Jennifer's hand as they were being told what to expect. He wanted to say that they'd take both of them, but Jennifer had said just one to start. The poor little tikes. Valyn wanted to hug them until they were better.

"What killed their father? And what did he do for a living?" Tholan looked at him and he nodded. "I asked the question, Tholan. I'm expecting you to answer me despite what Valyn says to protect me. Please tell me."

"The father was a drug dealer who would sell his sons

for money for his own addiction. I'm sorry, my lady. When he was killed, there was speculation that one of boys had done it. He was killed with a single gunshot to the head." She asked him who had done it. "The child. I think that is why he's having such a hard time with all this. He killed his father, no matter the circumstances."

"When can we have them? Today?" Valyn was so happy in that moment that he could have danced. But he wasn't going to until Tholan left. "I'd like to have enough time to get the bedrooms ready for them. Or should they be in one?"

"I think one for now." Tholan bowed before her and smiled when he stood up and continued. "You're much braver and stronger than people give you credit for. I'm proud to know you."

Valyn called out to Lily and to the other women of the Mystics. Neither Jennifer or he knew the first thing about buying things for two small children. When Lily told the others that she had it, she came to their home and smiled.

"I had high hopes that you'd take them both. I've heard that they are very fearful. And they won't allow anyone to touch them." Valyn asked her what she knew, hoping she had a little more information than Tholan. "What I can tell you is that it will take a great deal of love and understanding for them to come around to love you both. Starting off this way, to have children come into your home, this is the worst kind. But I have faith in you to do them good."

The shopping spree was much easier than he had thought it would be. Knowing their age and an approximate weight for them helped a great deal in getting clothing. Lily cautioned them not to go overboard at first. That would more than likely overwhelm them, and they'd had enough of that.

Beds were purchased to be delivered to his home. They were also going to have them assembled and made up while they were gone. Galin had said that he'd help them and watch the men coming to make sure that they didn't wander around too much. Valyn, like all of them, had a lot of antiques. Most of them had been used by him at some point in his life, and he didn't want them to get broken.

The clothing was harder to judge for them. Not the sizes, though they were guessing at them for the most part, but what each of them would like. Lily told them that since they'd had so very little when they were found, she had nothing to go on for styles or colors. Jennifer told him that she had it.

It only took her an hour to purchase the things that the kids would need. Shirts and pants, as well as coats. Socks were easy enough, he thought, and when she made her way to the toy department, he reminded her what Lily had told them.

"I know. But when I was a child, pretty much in the same position these two are in, minus the dead father, there were only a few things that I dearly wanted. And at the age of four, you can bet that he'd like something to hold close to his heart. Not a teddy bear, but something else." They walked up and down the aisles several times before she moved quickly up the next one. "This is what he needs. Now for Connor."

Connor was much harder to decide on. He wasn't a teenager yet, not for a few more years, but he'd had to grow up fast in order to keep him and his brother safe from people. Valyn was able to find just the thing for him when they were about ready to give up. They decided not to have them wrapped, but would give them to them when they were alone. Valyn drove them home slowly, thinking that in a few hours or less they'd be responsible for two little beaten children.

When the car pulled up in front of the house later that afternoon, they were about as ready as they could be. The rooms were plain, ready for them to decide on what they wanted. He knew that it would be a while before they trusted them with that sort of thing, but he was willing to wait them out. He had a lot of experience with children like these.

Connor came in the room first, followed right behind by Davy. Neither of them moved beyond the threshold, but Jennifer got down on her knees in front of them both. Saying nothing to either of them, she looked as if she was looking them over.

"My name is Jennifer. But you can call me Jenny if you'd like." Connor asked how long they had to stay here. "Why? Don't you think we'd take good care of you? Or are you planning your escape even though we've gone to a great deal of trouble to be ready for you?"

"We were doing all right by ourselves. I don't know why they made arrangements for us like we're stupid or something." Davy mimicked his brother on the last few words. "You guys are going to split us up, and that ain't happening. He's my brother, and I'm taking good care of him."

"Well of course you are. I shudder to think what would have happened to you should you have been found by someone unsavory. You must have been quick on your feet to have been able to feed each of you too, I think." Connor puffed out his chest and Jennifer went back to telling them what they'd be gaining by staying here. "There is enough food here that you don't have to ever go hungry again. There is a butler in the house, as well as a cook. And they are excited to have you here as well."

"What are they going to make us do to have food?" Jennifer looked at Valyn, then at Connor again. "I'm not going to do nothing with them. I won't do that again."

"No, you will not." Valyn got down to be on the same level as them. "You will never be the slave to someone so long as I have breath in my body. And that is forever, as I will not die."

"You have to die. Everyone does." Valyn knew this was risky, but he wanted them to be aware of what he was from the beginning. Trust, that's what he wanted them to have, and in him. When he stood up, he let his wings go and felt them spread out behind him. "What are you? An angel?"

Davy moved a couple of steps closer to him. And when he put out his shaky hand to touch him, Valyn moved so that he could. He could feel the child's hunger. Not just for food, but for someone to care for him.

"I'm what you call a Protector. Or I used to be one. Now I'm a Mystic, someone that helps others like me look

131

like everyone else when they're here." Connor touched the wings too, and from him he could feel the distrust, the pain he was in despite being taken care of in the hospital. "There are as many of my kind in the world as there are creatures in this world. Someone is with you from the time you are born and take your first breath to the very last one that you'll breathe. They help you, try to protect you in ways that you might not know of."

"Why didn't they protect us from those men? Why did they not help us when my dad was beating us and starving us?" Valyn pulled his wings to him and reached out for the boy. When he pulled back, he took him to his chest anyway. "Let me go. I don't like to be touched."

"No, you do like to be touched—you don't like to be hurt. I will never do that to you. As far as Jennifer and I are concerned, you are our sons and we will get hugs from you whenever we can." Slowly Connor started to weaken. He was tired of fighting, Valyn knew that. Sick of trying to stay safe for his little brother. "Your Protector was there with you when your father was. He said to tell you that every time you were able to hide from your father, every time that he took your supper from you, he whispered in your ear where to find something to eat for you both. He also hid you as much as he could."

Connor pulled away to look him in the face. There was a moment there when he thought that he'd won him over. But it was short lived, as the boy had more distrust than most people. Then when he moved back to his brother's side, he watched them both. It would take a while to have this child feel safe around them.

"Come on now. We didn't know what you'd like, so we have pizza for you. There is milk too, chocolate or white, and juice." Jennifer moved toward the kitchen without the boys. When she turned to them, asking them if they were coming with her, Connor looked at him again.

"I don't like you." Valyn told him that was all right for now. "And what if I run away and take Davy with me? Are you going to tie me up and then beat me? I won't let you."

"I've told you this before—I won't harm you like that. But if you do run away, I'd hope that you'd give us a chance to make up for whatever we've done to upset you." Connor wasn't buying it. Not that he blamed him. "How about we discuss this after dinner? I don't know about you guys, but I've been hungry since I found out what we were having."

He didn't put out his hand to guide them with him. Nor did he look back as he made his way to the kitchen. It was their decision to make, he supposed, but he was going to be very hurt if they ran away so soon.

The pizza was just coming out of the oven when he entered. Jennifer just looked at him and he shrugged. When the door swung open he held his breath to see if it was them or someone else coming in. It was the boys, and Davy looked like he'd been crying. Valyn asked them what they wanted to drink, and acted like it was nothing unusual for them to have children there.

"I want some milk. Please?" Jennifer asked Davy if he wanted white or chocolate. "I don't know what that is. I only ever had white, and it wasn't all that good. It tasted bad, but it was all we were allowed to drink."

133

Janie, their cook, huffed at him before speaking. "I milked the cow myself just this morning. I know that 'tis fresh. Next, if you want to be sure of its freshness, you can go down to the barn with me and watch me milk Sassy. She's a little on the grumpy side most days, but we get along."

The milk was poured into two different glasses. Janie mixed the chocolate syrup in one glass and plain milk was put in the other. Handing them to the boys, Janie told them to eat up or the pie would be too cold to eat soon. Davy picked up the first slice of the pizza and moaned when he chewed it up.

"I never had hot pizza before. Have we, Connor? We would have to steal it from the trash when it was there. But this is really good." Davy ate his piece and was on his second one when Connor reached out and took one. He didn't say anything, but Valyn could tell that he was glad for it. As they sat there, talking about nothing, the boys filled their bellies with not just pizza, but a plate of grapes as well as peach pie. They were nearly asleep on their feet as they took them up to their room.

"I've put you both in this room for now. If you decide that you want to have separate rooms, we have the other one set up for whomever." Jennifer helped Davy put his new pajamas on and brush his teeth. This too was a new experience for them. It was no wonder they were so beaten, not even to have simple things like pajamas and a toothbrush. "Now, tomorrow we'll show you around the house. There aren't any rooms that are off limits to you so long as you're careful of the things in each room. All right?"

"You'll beat us if we break anything, right?" Jennifer told him no, they weren't going to be beaten. "Then you'd better tell us what you want with us. I'm telling you, I won't do nothing with you. Never again. So you can just fuck off if that's what you're thinking."

Jennifer smacked him across the mouth. It wasn't hard, but she had his full attention now. Connor stiffened when she reached for him. But instead of letting him flinch away from her, she pulled him onto her lap.

"I don't know exactly what sort of life you lived before coming here with us, but we do not use that sort of language when we're here. We're trying our best here, and all you've done is push us further and further back. We've told you, several times, that we will not beat you. But that doesn't mean that we won't discipline you when you need it." Jennifer turned Connor's face up so that she could see it. "You're a good boy, I know that. And I know some of the things that were done to you. I can't imagine what you had to do to make yourself stay alive all this time. That's more than any adults would have done, I think, under the same circumstances."

"He hated us. And we had to run off when it was bad." Jennifer held him to her bosom and rocked back and forth. "I killed him for us. It wasn't Davy like them other people think. It was all me, and if I have to go to prison for it, I don't want Davy hurt."

"No one cares that he's dead, no matter who killed him. He was a hurtful, mean man, and he didn't deserve to have someone like you two in his life. That's why we wanted

135

you to come here. We want you to be not just a part of our lives, but to be happy and carefree while you're here." She kissed him on the nose and helped him back in bed. "Now, no more talking about beatings or going to prison. No one will harm either of you, not over my dead body. And let me tell you, I'm one tough woman."

When they left the room, they were both talking quietly. Valyn asked them if they wanted the light on or off and they both said on. Monsters were still lurking around them, and a light, he thought, could keep them at bay.

Valyn joined Jennifer in the living room. It was going to be harder than he thought to take on children if they were all like these two. But he'd have it no other way. He was going to make this work if he had to work on it day and night. Laughing, he wondered what he'd think about that comment in about a week. He hoped it wouldn't be a problem. He hoped.

~*~

Beth didn't understand why her daughter had to move so far away from her. Of course, she was glad to have her out of her hair after she turned about eight or something. Life was too much fun to have a child hanging onto you for every little thing.

She'd kept up with her over the years. Not really looking for her or anything, but she'd see her name in the paper about this and that. The diner incident had her believing her daughter was just like her — taking out the bad guy to look like a hero and maybe getting some cash while she was at it. But she soon found out that the man had killed other people in the place, and Jenny hadn't only saved her own ass but the entire diner full of people. Nothing like her momma would do. She was more into looking out for only herself and she'd be just fine.

The next time she'd seen her name—well, somebody else had seen it and showed it to her—Jenny had gotten married, to some rich fucker that she was sure her little girl was going to run dry. But that didn't happen either. She was turning out to be a Miss Goody Two-Shoes about the credit cards someone was taken out in someone else's name. A credit card scam of all things. She wished she'd have thought of that. And Jenny had not even taken a dime of it for herself. Nor a finder's fee for her work.

"Stupid brat. She never did learn the value of money. Always wanting to put it away for something." Beth snorted and looked around to see if she had any more coke left. "I'll show her just how to make life a happy ending. She'll fork over some money or I'll tell Daddy Money Bags that she's not whatever he thinks she is."

Snorting some more up her nose, she laid back on the couch that she'd been crashing on for the last few weeks. She was getting the hint that the couple that she'd known for some years didn't like her as much as they used to. Changed, they had, and she hated them for being so stuck up all the time. They had had all the fun sucked right out of them because they had a few kids. Well, she'd taken care of hers. Beth often wondered why they hadn't done the same thing.

Soon she was going to head out and make her way to Ohio. Hitching rides as much as she could. Beth had a nice sleeping bag that she'd stolen a few months back and some jerky to eat on the way. Whatever happened, Beth figured she was ready for it. And if not, then so the fuck what. She was living the good life.

Beth heard someone on the stairs and tried to cover up the mess that she'd made on the coffee table.

"Beth, you told me that you'd be out of here first thing in the morning. That was five days ago. You're going to have to get your act together and get out. I've told you several times, we don't live that life any longer, and we don't care for you bringing that stuff in the house either. I have children now." Margo tossed her backpack at her and said to pack it up. "I want you out of here within the hour, or I'm going to have to evict you with the polices' help."

"You sure have changed your tune, Margo. What happened to the woman who could get as high as a kite and still drive home in a reasonably safe way? At least you didn't hit too many things while you were at it." Margo told her that she wasn't twenty any more. "No, you sure ain't. And you look like it's passed you by at least three times over."

"And how do you think you look, Beth? Your hair hasn't been washed in months. I'm betting that your body hasn't either. And no matter how many times I've scrubbed the couch, your smell just will not go away. I'm going to have to burn it as soon as you leave." Beth laughed at Margo and her woes. "You look your age too, only you look as if you've been run over several times and left to die. That is not a good look on anyone. Especially on a fifty-year-old hippie who thinks the world owes her."

"I'm nowhere near being fifty. You just want to make

yourself look good." Margo told her what her birthdate was, as well as the year she was born. Then she counted it out for her. "Well, with that sort of logic, I guess you must be right. But the thing is, I don't feel it. Not once have I looked back on my life and thought I'd do it different like. Nope, I'm really happy with everything I did back then and now."

"I want you out of here now." Beth stood up and was going to slap Margo into shutting up, but she was either too stoned to do it or she tripped over something. Ending up on the floor face down didn't feel right. "I'm calling the police. Let them deal with your skanky ass."

Skanky? No one had ever called her that before. Not that she'd been aware of anyway. She might have put a smackdown on them had she known about it. But Margo had been her friend for a long time. And now she was doing this. *Makes a girl hate to have friends*, Beth thought.

"I'm leaving." Beth got up and looked around for her stuff. She was sure that she'd come here with more than a little backpack. "Where are my things? Are you stealing from me now?"

"There is nothing that you have that I would even touch, much less steal from you. You're just nasty, Beth. And I hope when you find Jennifer, you get what's coming to you." Beth told Margo that she was going to give her the keys to the castle when she found her. "I hope she uses those keys to lock you up. That poor girl went through a lot when you left her standing on the side of the road after hitching a ride with a stranger. Why would you do something like that?"

"He, like me, didn't want to be hauling around a kid all the time when we were going to have some fun. What should I have done, Margo, let her get high with us? Maybe let her blow the man for the ride? No thanks, he was mine." Margo asked her if she even remembered the man's name. "Don't remember, only that he had himself a nice dick that he knew how to use. And by the time I figured out that he was not for me, I couldn't remember where I left her or nothing."

She was slowly making her way to the door. The sooner she got on the road again, the sooner she'd have some money. Turning to ask her old friend for a buck or two, the door slammed in her face. Christ, what a cunt Margo had turned out to be.

Walking in the snow wasn't easy. *Not while you're stoned*, she thought with a giggle. And the fact that her boots leaked like a sieve didn't help matters none. By the time she'd made her way to the highway, she was shivering again, and her feet were soaking wet. *What a way to go on*, she thought.

Beth tried to think of anything else but the cold and wet. She decided to think about the money that Jenny would be forking over. And she'd better too. Being her momma had better bring her some perks from her daughter marrying a rich bastard.

She really hadn't been a good mom. Not that anyone cared about it. Jenny had been a pain in the ass, from the moment that she came screaming out of her to the minute Beth left her standing there. Jenny had had the most crushed look on her face. When she needed a good laugh,

Beth would think of her little face.

Over the years she'd thought about her daughter. What she was doing, if she had a place for her momma to crash for a few months. But Beth had never really pursued finding her until she was desperate. And that happened more times than she cared to think about. There was a couple of times that she'd find her number and call her. They'd meet someplace and then Jenny would tell her to leave her alone, she had a good life now. Beth was never invited to her home, she only just realized. Probably thought that she would take her things again, which she would.

There had been money for her then too. A fifty here and a twenty there. Sometimes she'd give her a hundred, but that soon dried up too. Jenny wanted her to get clean and find a job. Beth had told her that she had a job, taking money from her. That had been the last time she'd given over anything, including a lunch like she used to buy her when they were together.

Thumbing for a ride had always been easy for her when she was younger. The years, she knew without Margo pointing it out, had not been kind to her. Other than the nasty hair that she said she had, Beth didn't care if she was clean or not. It was the way she liked to live. On the side of danger. Laughing, she put out her thumb for the trucks that passed her by.

It was nearly midnight when she walked to the rest stop. It felt like she'd been walking for hours and hours, but she knew that it had only been a couple of them. She wasn't cut out to be walking anywhere. She should have a man to cart her ass around. But those too were few and far between since she'd gotten a bit older.

Getting a ride from one of the truckers had cost her a blow job for him. Not that she minded them, but some men could be real pigs when it was time to pay up. But Beth was getting smarter. She'd only blow them when they were in the truck. That way he couldn't leave her stranded after she'd done her part.

Beth asked him how long before they hit the little town outside of a stupid town called Zanesville. "How could anyone live in a place called that? It must take them ten minutes to write it out when they need to. They should call it something short. Like one of them other towns in that area. Sure would be nice if they made things easier on a person instead of hard."

Having no idea what she'd been talking about in the first place, Beth laid her head on the window and decided to let her buzz take her to bed. Smiling, she thought of the look on Jenny's face when Beth showed up out of the blue. She sure was going to be fit to be tied when she did.

It wasn't going to be a homecoming so much as a war between them. Beth knew it too. She'd have to convince her that she'd changed, and then put out her hand for her to fill it. And she'd better fill it to the top, by God, or she was going to get medieval on her ass.

Laughing at the thought of trying to beat her daughter's ass, Beth decided to let sleep take her under. She had to look good for her son-in-law if nothing else. This was going to be epic, Beth knew it. And if her daughter wouldn't pony up, she'd work on the husband. Surely, he'd want his mother-in-law to be set up, wouldn't he? Beth hoped so. Life was gonna be difficult on them if they didn't.

CHAPTER 10

Jenny was sitting at the kitchen table when the boys came down to the dining room. Neither of them was dressed in the new clothes, but were wearing the same things they'd come here in. But she did notice that Davy had on the shoes she'd gotten for him. Standing up, she helped him into the chair, then pulled out one for Connor.

"I'm only having tea and a scone for breakfast. What do you guys want? We have cereal if you want that. Or Janie can cook you something hot. We have a lot to do today, and I was hoping you guys would get up early, so we can get started." Davy asked what they were going to be doing. But she could tell that Connor was just as curious. "While you guys eat, I'll give you a rundown. Go ahead, tell her what you want."

Davy asked for bacon. That was all, just bacon. And when asked about and egg or toast, he nodded and asked her if that was all right. Janie huffed. She was really good at that, Jenny thought.

143

"You can have whatever I have in my pantry. I was thinking of baking some cookies up today too. I like them warm right out of the oven with a cup of tea, myself. What do you guys think of chocolate chip?" Davy again was the one who answered, and he gave her a resounding yes on that. "Good. I'll make sure I time it right for when you'll be back." Connor said he just wanted cereal.

"Today we're going to see about getting you something else to wear, first of all. I know that some of the things that we got didn't fit. We'll remedy that first." She drank a sip of her tea to hide the smile at the look on Connor's face. He was staring at Davy's breakfast like a man on the edge. A bowl and a box of colorful cereal was put in front of him. "Then we have to go by the grocery store for a few things. Connor, you can pick yourself out some different cereals if you want that for breakfast from now on."

"No, I think I'll have what Davy is eating. It looks all right." Janie, the huffing queen, scooped up the bowl and box and replaced it with a plate full of the same thing that Davy had. Bacon, eggs, fluffy pancakes, and a bowl of fruit. "I'll eat this, I guess." And he did, every last crumb of it.

By the time she got them both bundled up and in the car, she was ready for a nap. It was an uphill battle trying to make sure that they were dressed in good sturdy clothing, as well as hats, gloves, and coats. Jenny wasn't sure what she would have done if Janie hadn't helped her.

The drive to the mall was made slowly. There was fresh snow on the ground, despite it being the beginning of February. And when they arrived, Davy had to go to the bathroom. That was where she thought she might fail them.

"I'll take him." She thanked Connor, and told him how much she appreciated his help. And when they left her to go into the men's room, she wanted to bar others from going in with them. She was afraid for them, she thought, and didn't want anything to happen to them. When they finally came out, she got down on her knees and helped Davy with his pants, all the while talking to Connor.

"Do you like comics, Connor?" He said that he'd never had one. "Oh well, we'll go by the comic store too while we're here. I know that Valyn loves them. He has a collection that is very old. Maybe you can have him show it to you."

"Whatever."

She wanted to lash out at him, tell him that she was trying her best here, but moved to pull them both along to the first store. Jenny was hurt, and she knew that was what Connor had planned to do to her.

They spent about three hours in the clothing store before she realized how late it was. Going to the mall area that had restaurants, she had no idea what they would like. She asked Connor what he wanted, and he looked at the burger place. Davy wanted a taco, even though he had not one clue what it was.

"If I give you money, do you think you can walk over there and order your food?" Connor looked terrified and shook his head no. "All right then. We'll go and get you yours first, and then when you're at a table, I'll get mine and Davy's. Is that all right?"

"Don't go too far." She nodded. "I mean with Davy. I

don't want you going too far away with my brother. I need him."

"I promise you that I won't go far. So long as you sit at the table and don't leave it. I don't want to lose you here. It's very busy." He nodded, and they made their way over to the restaurant.

She ordered for him and paid. He was afraid of her leaving him, she only just realized. And when he was handed his food on a tray, he looked at her like he was lost. Taking it from him, she talked about anything that popped into her head as she found them a table close to the taco place.

Jenny tried very hard not to keep looking for Connor every few minutes. But true to his word, he never left the table. And when she and Davy joined him, he helped with his brother's food and then his own. She supposed that he was used to caring for him, and even now it was habit.

Connor ate the burger in no time. He might have been eating while he could, or he was that hungry, she didn't know. But when she offered to get him another burger, he nodded and smiled at her. Jenny could have gone a lifetime on the feelings that it invoked in her.

Returning with the burger, she noticed a couple watching them. For some reason they gave her the creeps, and she wanted to take the kids to her chest and warn them off. But she only sat there, eating her lunch and enjoying the conversation of the kids. Then the couple came to their table. Connor reached for her hand and she took it.

"We wanted to tell you how wonderful your children are." She nodded her thanks and waited for one of them to tell the couple they weren't hers. "They're so polite and helpful to each other. You and your husband must be really proud of them. Good job. I wish more people would take lessons from you."

When they wandered off, she let go of Connor's hand when he pulled it. She sat there for several minutes before she started laughing. Davy joined her, but Connor just stared at her. She finally had to stop laughing so they'd not call the cops on her.

"I thought for sure she was going to take you guys. I have no idea why, but I have to tell you, I was going to smack them around a lot if they even touched either of you." Connor asked her why she'd not just let them have the two of them. "Why? Because even though you've only been with us for a day, I love you two with all my heart. You're just what we wanted in children to come to us. I wish that I could have taken you sooner, but we're family now, and that's what's important to me."

Jenny was worried about how Connor would take it, but she gathered them up again to go to the next store. He didn't say anything about it again and she let it go. Davy became a chatterbox of all kinds of information, and she got a kick out of some of the words he stumbled over.

By the time they had gotten all they could stuff in the car, they left the mall. It was nearly dinnertime then, and she asked Valyn if he wanted to join them in town. He was thrilled, telling her that he'd not had such a good day and could use something different than work right now. This time the dinner menu was a restaurant that prided itself on not just steaks, but also their milkshakes.

Valyn kissed her and gave her a hug, then turned to the boys. He asked if he could get a hug and Davy seemed to jump into his arms. Connor was a little less enthusiastic about it, but he let Valyn hug him in the end. They were seated in a booth with Davy on the side of Valyn and Connor near her.

Today she had learned a great deal about each of their boys. For one, Connor was smart. Very smart if what he was telling her about some of the books he'd read was true. He also loved math, and was right on top of it when they were buying things. He'd tell her how much it should come to before tax, and he'd be spot on when they paid.

Davy was a jokester. He enjoyed slapstick mostly, but he liked a good joke too. He wasn't very good at telling them, but he did try. Davy also loved books. And even for as young as he was, he could read very well. Which reminded her, they needed to get them into a school. Watching them talk to and tell Valyn about their day, she leaned back on the seat and just enjoyed being with them.

Even though the day had been trying at times, she wouldn't have missed it for the world. And the fact that they were much better at talking to them, it had made it easier to get them clothing that they liked instead of what she had already bought them.

When they were walking out to their car, Valyn coming with them because Galin had just dropped him off, she remembered the gifts that they'd gotten them. And she was proud that what they'd gotten them was a good choice. As soon as they got home, she was going to give them to the boys. It was an exciting time for them all.

Driving had become scary now. The snow was covering the road and there was slush everywhere the snow wasn't. Cars were taking heed of the weather and driving slowly. When they came to the town's only stop light, she let out a long breath that they'd made it nearly home without incident.

"I'll be glad to get home." She told Valyn that she would be as well and turned to make sure the boys were buckled in good and tight. "There are a lot of fools out tonight too. Look how fast that guy is going. He'll be lucky to make it home at that speed."

Valyn pulled out into the traffic when the light turned green. She had only just gotten her license the other day, so she was sure that they were all right with Valyn driving. Jenny saw the car coming at them, and the look of pure terror on the man's face that was going to hit them.

The first jolt of the car being hit had her nearly sick with the pain. She had bumped her head on the window and knew that she was going to have a headache from it. The second time they were hit, she knew a new kind of fear — her sons were in the back seat, and that was where the second car had hit them.

Screaming at them to hold on, that they had them, she knew things were off when she kept seeing the road then the sky in alternating sparks of color. They were flipping over now, and she knew they were all going to be hurt badly.

Jenny woke when someone called her name. It was hard to hear anything with the buzzing in her head. When she finally was able to move enough to turn toward the voice, she saw Valyn there. She cried when she saw that he was alive. But Jenny wanted to know about their sons.

"Davy? Connor?" Valyn said for her to come to him so that he could get her out of the vehicle. "Where are the boys? Where are my boys, Valyn?"

"They've been taken to the hospital. I thought that they should have care first, honey. You're an immortal. You can be hurt, and you are, but I don't know if they are or not." He was crying when they got her out of the car, and she asked him how they were. "Davy is hurt, but Connor took the brunt of the car hitting us. He's hurt very badly."

"Take me to them." He nodded and helped her to lie back on the ground when she got too dizzy to stand. "Please, I have to make sure that they're all right. I need to be with them."

"The ambulance is taking you there now. I'm going to be in there with you. We'll get to them soon, love. We'll get there." She didn't like that he kept looking away. Jenny knew that they were hurt much more than he was telling her.

Jenny didn't ask again, fearful that he'd tell her the horrid truth, that Connor was going to die. Or worse yet, they had both died and that they'd lost them even before they got to tell them how much she already loved them.

Valyn held her hand all the way to the hospital. She wanted them to take her right to their boys, but they wanted to make sure that she was going to be all right first. Jenny had never thought of time going too slowly, but right now, it seemed the second hand was taking several seconds to move and not the usual one.

Valyn went to check on the boys while she let the doctor examine her. When he came back, she knew that he had bad news for her. And when he laid his forehead to hers, she started sobbing. She'd been too late. Connor was gone, and she hurt like she'd never hurt before.

"Connor's in surgery." She asked him what he said. "He is in surgery now. To repair the three broken ribs he has from poking his lungs. And he has a broken arm. Davy is all right—he's coming with the nurse who was watching over them."

Davy was there—she didn't hear him come in, the doctor having given her something for the pain. So, when she woke, Davy was lying next to her in the bed and Valyn was in the chair next to them. Touching Davy's blond hair, she cried again because they had let them get hurt.

~*~

Connor was hurting more than he ever had after the beatings that his father would give him. But he was alive. He'd thought they were all goners when that car plowed into them like they were only a bump in the road. Taking in his surroundings, he saw that he had a cast on his arm and his left ankle was wrapped up. But it was his breathing that hurt him the most.

"Hey, buddy." He looked up at Valyn and asked about Davy. "He's with Jennifer. She is in another room on a different floor. I'm working to get her down here too."

Connor nodded and asked if he could have a drink. When the straw was put in his mouth, he felt like he'd been given the best stuff in the world. Valyn told him to go slowly, he still had some injuries that needed to heal. When

Connor nodded because he was still dry, Valyn took the straw away and took his hand in his.

"How are you feeling, buddy? I can tell you where you're hurt if you want. You have several broken ribs from the crash. And in turn, you had one or two of them that pushed into your lung. Are you with me so far?" He said that he was. "Good boy. The doctor said that you have a turned ankle that needed to be wrapped, as well as a few dozen places on your face that needed to be stitched up. And of course, as you can see, a broken arm. The cuts are not too bad, but they might leave you a tiny scar."

"And Mom, how is she?" He knew that she wasn't his mom, but he'd heard her when the car was rolling over. She'd called to them to hold on, telling them that she loved them. "She saved us. Telling me to hold on. I grabbed Davy and held him tight."

"Mom? Well, the police are saying you more than likely saved Davy from being more hurt than he was. There are a few places on his arm that needed stitches, but other than some scratches on his body from the car being flipped over, he's fine." Valyn put his head to his, and Connor could see that he was crying. "I've never been so afraid in my life as when they pulled you from the wreckage. I told you that I'd keep you safe, and I failed you both."

Connor had never hugged anyone before but his brother, but when he put his good arm around the big man, he felt something that tore at his heart a bit. The man had been upset that they'd been hurt. He didn't think that anyone had ever felt that way about them in all his life. Holding him for a little while more, Connor let him go when he stood up.

"Your mom, she's pretty beat up too. But she's begging—no, demanding—that they let her come and see you. She said that she's going to kick some butt if they don't give her a wheelchair and let her go. She— Her face looks bad, but it'll heal soon. And she does have some deep cuts along her legs where the glass hit her. That's why they're keeping her overnight. I've been running back and forth between you and her since you were brought in. Are you really okay?"

"I'm better now that I know they're okay." Connor got another sip of water and it still tasted delicious. "That guy that hit us, he was going really fast, wasn't he? I mean, he hit us more than once, right?"

"No, but he did cause the accidents. After he hit us, we were thrown into traffic and hit by other cars that were there. I think the police said that there were six cars in all that had been damaged in some way. I'm just glad that you two were in the back and buckled in." He grinned then. "Your mother is going to have a fit, just so you know. All the things that she bought for you guys are all over the road and have been run over a few dozen times."

"I know that you're not a human, you showed us that. But I have to tell you something. A secret. I saw a few of them there, people with wings, when we were being knocked around. I thought for sure they were coming for us all." He closed his eyes and knew that he'd been given something for pain. He pried his eyes open to look at Valyn the best he could. "Thank you, Dad, for being here with me. Nobody else would have but you and Mom."

153

For the first time in all his life, Connor knew that he could rest easy, that no one would hurt him or his brother. He knew that he'd been hurt, but it was the other guy's fault, not Dad's. Sleep seemed to just swallow him whole.

The next time he woke up, he saw his mom sitting in the chair in front of him. She did look bad. Her face was swollen, and she had a puffy lip on the top. Her hair, usually pulled back in some kind of clippie thing, was hanging down, and it made her look younger. Right now she was sleeping, but he knew that if he even breathed hard, she'd be awake. Looking around the room, he saw Davy was staring at him from Valyn's lap. Getting up quietly, he came to stand next to the bed.

"You hurting, Connor?" He whispered that he was going to be all right. "I was scared out of my pants when you grabbed me up like you did."

"Mom told me to hold on, and you were the first person I thought of holding. You didn't get too hurt, did you?" Davy showed him the cuts on his arm and the stitches that were a bright green. "Those will have the girls all over you."

"Yuck." He smiled at his little brother and it hurt a little. Connor had to be careful the next time. "You called her Mom. Is that what I should call her too? She's not, you know. She's much nicer."

"I'm going to. She saved our lives, and Valyn said that it scared him nearly to death when they pulled us out of the car." Davy said it did him too. "They didn't get mad or blame us for the accident. Dad would have. He would have said something like, 'Damned kids, they made me do it.'"

154

Davy giggled, then tried to climb in the bed with him. Valyn lifted him up, and after telling him to be careful, he covered them both up. Davy told him that he loved him so much. And Connor told him that he kinda liked him. It was what they always said to each other.

Mom woke up soon after, and started sobbing about how sorry she was and that she almost didn't get to tell them that she loved them. All kinds of things were spilling out of her mouth like the tears on her cheeks. He looked at Dad, and he just told him she needed it. Whatever that meant. But he did let her hold and kiss him. It was great having someone get all mushy with him. Another first for him.

At suppertime Valyn was able to sneak him in a milkshake. He'd never had one of those before. Davy liked his, but when given a drink of Dad's he wanted a malt the next time. When the nurse brought him in his dinner, she fussed at Dad for spoiling his dinner.

After they all went to bed, right there in the room with him, Connor thought about today. He wasn't sure if he should believe his good luck or not. No one had ever been nice to him and Davy, not even the teachers at the school they'd been going to.

He looked over when Mom touched his hand.

"Can't sleep?" He said he was tired, but his body wasn't. "That's the shock of what happened to you. We were all very lucky yesterday. I've never been frightened like that before. That driver, he wasn't paying attention like he should have been."

"Is he all right? Valyn said that there were other cars

in the accident. Are all those people all right too?" She told him that the driver had died from his injuries, and one of the passengers from one of the other cars was ejected from it because they'd not had on a seatbelt. "That's a shame. All those people have been hurt or killed because someone wanted to go too fast."

"I wanted to talk to you about some things, if you don't mind."

He thought that she was going to tell him she'd changed her mind and that she didn't want them. He started thinking of ways to change her mind back. Connor started crying and telling her that they'd be better if she'd not let them take them. And that he'd make sure that he and Davy were bathed every night. He said that he'd even eat yucky food if she'd only let them stay. Please.

"Connor, I'm not giving you away." He asked her if she was sure. "Yes, I'm very sure. I love you, and I don't.... Why, I don't think I could give you away under any circumstances. You and your brother are our children, and we want you to stay forever if you wish it."

"I want to stay. I want to be your son, and I want you to give me hugs all the time." He wiped at his tears. "I've never had anyone around me that didn't hit or beat me with a belt. I remember my mom. She would do just about anything to keep from being around us. I think that's why she left us. My dad said it was our fault that she did."

"I don't know why your mom left you there—I could never do that. But whatever her reasons were, it's her loss and our gain to have you in our lives." She took his hand into hers and kissed it. "I wanted to talk to you about school. And if you wanted to go back to the same place or not."

"I don't. They were mean to me and Davy because they said we smelled. I tried to clean us up the best I could, but they still didn't like us. Davy didn't want to go to preschool anymore because he said his teacher made him sit far away from the other kids." Mom asked him her name. "Mrs. Dufrene. She was the meanest of them all. And the principle made us stand in the hall sometimes when the other kids would make fun of us. Her name was Mrs. Cochran."

"You won't have to worry about them then. We'll put you in a different school as soon as you're able." She smiled at him, and he was sort of afraid of her for a minute. "I'll take care of Mrs. Dufrene and Mrs. Cochran."

Connor almost felt sorry for the other two women. His new mom, she sure did look like she could take on the whole school and come out on top. He sure hoped she did — he was getting used to having a full belly and warm feet.

CHAPTER 11

Beth was let out of the truck about ten miles from the little town. The fucker wouldn't even give her the money to make a fucking call to her daughter. Told her that he'd had enough of her sucking up his air and breathing out that nasty shit she'd been eating.

Beth moved along the road and saw the lights of a city up ahead. Oh, to be warm and full again. To be high wouldn't be remiss either. That had been the word of the day on Margo's calendar, remiss. And she'd been able to use it twice now. As she trudged through the snow to who the fuck knew where, she thought about all the things she was going to say to Jenny when she saw her. And if that didn't work, she'd go see the husband. He must have been a real wiener to be marrying her daughter.

The snow was building up now and she could no longer feel her feet. She thought that she's read someplace that if you couldn't feel your feet, then you were frosted. Or something like that. She only knew that she was fucking freezing and she wanted to sit down.

The car came out of nowhere, and she had to leap out of the way of it or be run down. The son of a bitch had nearly killed her, and then he turned and flipped her off. If she had a gun right now, she'd blow his fucking head off. Dangerous drivers made her sick. And she'd broken the heel off her boot. *Mother fuck, could this get any worse?* she thought.

The little town came into view about the time she was going to give up. There couldn't be any kid that was worth all this. But the money certainly was. Walking again, she had a thought; what if her daughter wasn't even home? Rich fucks went on vacations where it was warm when this shit started coming on. Pissed now, she stomped her way into the little stop and go store, just waiting to take it out on someone. But the smell of sizzling hot dogs had her mouth watering and her belly waking up in protest. Beth couldn't remember the last time she'd had anything to eat.

Lucky for her, or not, the woman behind the counter was too busy playing on her phone to give her any kind of look. Walking to the aisles that were furthest away from the counter, she pulled open her purse and put about half a dozen candy bars in it. Strolling around the other aisles, she picked herself up a few cookies, a lighter, as well as some kind of energy drink, thinking she could walk faster that way.

Phone watcher asked her if she needed anything. "Nah, I'm looking for a certain brand of candy bar, and I'm trying to jog my memory what it was by looking at them all."

The woman must have believed her because when she

sat down this time, her phone plastered to her face, she had her back to her. Hurrying over to the hot dog roller, she grabbed up a bag of the buns and eight or nine of the dogs. Pulling herself a drink out of the cooler, she figured she was set to go. Beth was nearly to the door when a cop in his cruiser pulled up in the front of the store.

"Hello, Mable. You having a good night?" Phone watcher just grunted at him, and Beth worked herself closer to the door when the cop stood in front of the counter. "I'll have three of them donuts and some coffee. I'll get it if you wrap me up the fresh ones."

He turned his back to her and Beth hurried out the door. She was nearly down the block before she thought she was far enough away to pull out something to eat. The dogs tasted like heaven to her, and she ate three of them while walking. Christ, this was more excitement than she'd had in a month of Sundays.

Now that she had her belly full and the pop drank, she was feeling sleepy. What she wouldn't give for a hit or two about now. That would mellow her out enough that she could sleep about anywhere. But since there wasn't any on her, she had to settle for sleeping in the garage that had been left open.

There were a couple of old blankets on the top shelf of a rack. Pulling them down on top of her nearly knocked her out when something heavy come tumbling off onto her. After making sure that she wasn't bleeding, Beth laid one of the blankets on the floor and the other one across her. It wasn't perfect, but she was out of the cold and snow and in the town, she hoped, that Jenny was in.

Morning came all too quickly for her. In fact, Beth hadn't seen a morning in more years than she hadn't. She wasn't a morning person. And without something to tide her over, she was a bitch too. When she heard voices on the other side of the car, that woke her ass up. She covered herself from head to toe in the blanket and hoped they weren't that observant.

The two of them, a man and woman, must have said goodbye to each other a million times. It was to the point that she was going to get up and tell him to get out of here, for Christ's sake. When he did pull out, finally, she heard the door go down. Good thing she'd not tried that last night or she would have woken everyone within a block up. When it hit the concrete on the floor, she was plunged into complete darkness.

Sore and stiff, she worked out the kinks in her body a little at a time. She figured that since there was only one car in the garage she didn't have to worry about the woman coming out sometime and finding her. Beth ate two more of the hot dogs, stone cold now, as she contemplated her fate.

She had to find Jenny. That had to be a priority. Then she had to get her to hand over money. And a great deal of it. There wasn't any point in her having to come back here every few weeks for more. In fact, she thought that Jenny should just give her one of the credit cards she was sure that she had. Smiling, Beth liked that plan.

The side door to the garage wasn't locked, so she opened it quietly and looked around the garage for something to hock for some cash. She hadn't seen any taxis around, and wondered if this little burg even knew what they were. Finding nothing of value, she left the garage. But not before letting the people of the house know that they'd had a guest in their garage.

Beth hadn't spray painted her name on the art work, as she'd done before. That shit was what got her caught. Something about defacing some monument or some shit, Beth couldn't remember. She'd had to wash every drop of paint off of it before they'd let her go, too. And she was never to return. Not that she wanted to or anything, but she was more careful now.

Walking in the daylight had its advantages as well as disadvantages. For one, she could see where to avoid the puddles of water that seemed to be everywhere. Then there was the trouble with being seen around. Being vagrant, as she'd been called before, could get her a night or two in jail. She'd just as soon avoid that if she could.

Beth hadn't known anything about the town when she decided to come here. She figured that it was a one-horse town where everybody knew everybody's business. There was no way for her to tell about the latter of the two, but it was a pretty little place. Even the store that she'd been in last night looked good with the sun streaming over it.

Figuring that the rich fuck lived outside the town, she walked away from the library, not having any idea why, but she thought that she'd have luck going that way. She was nearly out of the town, to where there was nothing but fields of snow-covered broken stick-looking things, when she knew she'd made a mistake. She had to retrace her steps and head back in the other direction.

The houses did get bigger the more she walked. Some of them had long driveways and gates at the entrance. Big letters — she supposed it was their last name and that they were giving people a hint as to who might live there. It didn't help her; she couldn't remember the rich fuck's last name at all.

The biggest house of all was right in front of her, up one of them long assed driveways. She had no idea why she knew it was her daughter's, but Beth knew that it was. She watched the man at the gate, to see when he'd not be looking around. But the guy was either a statue or he was taking his job very seriously. He never looked down at all, even when he answered the phone. This was going to be tricky.

The need to get through the gates was something that she'd not thought of. Who the hell gated their driveway, unless they were drug dealers or pimps? Since she had no idea what the rich fuck did, she had to give him some kind of job, she thought, and gave him all kinds of notorious jobs just off the top of her head.

A car came down the drive and she backed away from it. There was a man at the wheel and a woman on her side of the car. She got a good look at her and was stunned when she finally realized it was Jenny. Christ, she had turned out better than she'd thought she would. She was beautiful.

When the gate started to close behind the car, she nearly missed her chance to go in without being detected. The guard was putting his trash in a can, she'd only just noticed, and she darted in as the gate was closing. By the time she was at the trees that lined up like soldiers along the drive, she was exhausted and a little sick to her belly. The hot dogs were not agreeing with her at the moment. All this running around was also giving her a major headache.

There wasn't a drop of snow on the driveway, like it was frowned upon to have snow there. She laughed, nearly falling over with it when she started talking in a posh voice and making exaggerated gestures with her hands. Stopping when she stood before the house, she could only stare.

"Christ almighty. She's hit the fucking jackpot. Look at this place." No one was around to catch her, but she didn't care. The house was what little girls dreamed up when they were thinking about a Prince Charming. Like there ever was one.

The huge assed wrap around porch had baskets of Christmas greenery on each of the poles that separated the railing, which seemed like it was made from glass, it was so beautiful. There were rockers as well, four on each side of the double doors at the front. She imagined that she'd find the same on the back, and more than likely a big pool too. The windows along the front, four on each side, were all topped with stained glass pictures, which she was too far away to make out.

A six-car garage that wasn't attached to the house looked like it had an apartment or something over it. She might even talk her daughter into letting her live up there for a time. It would be nice to have something that nice for a change.

Moving closer to the house, she noticed that not only was there greenery on the porch, but big barrels that would hold flowers, she'd bet, in the summer months. Pressing her face against the first window she came to, she could see furniture that was well maintained, as well as a big fireplace. She'd love to be sitting in front of that about now.

Careful of where she was, making sure that the guard hadn't figured out that she was here, she walked around the big house to see what was in the back yard. The pool that she'd imagined was there, but much bigger than she'd thought. And she saw a large house that had smoke coming from the stone chimney. A house for the cook, no doubt, she thought. Figures — her kid's help had more than she did at the moment. Beth wandered back around to the front of the house, pissed off now.

"I'm gonna have to make her see reason. She can either give me some cash or I'm going to go the newspapers around the area and have them slander her." Beth wasn't sure that was the right way to put it, but she knew what she meant. "Then we'll see how well she takes care of me. It doesn't matter none that I left her by the road. She did all right, didn't she? Bitch will be paying me, that's for damned sure."

Hiding in the trees on the opposite side of the cook's house, she decided that she'd take herself a little snooze in the garage. The trouble was, it was locked up tighter than anything she'd ever seen. After trying every door twice, she went back to the trees and sat on the ground, unmindful of her pants getting soaked.

Beth was pissed now. And when she was pissed off, she did stupid things. She knew this. It's what got her into trouble all the damned time. Getting up, she planned on busting out a window or two, so she could get in where it was warm, but she heard someone coming up the drive. She hid again. It wasn't the right time, she told herself, to be meeting her daughter.

~*~

Jenny fussed over Connor all the way back to the house. He finally told her to leave him be. Turning around, she had to smile. She had been bothering him too much. It was fun to see him try to be nice and tell her off at the same time. She loved these kids.

Jenny had never dreamed of being a mom. She'd had the worst of the worst, and the thought of messing up even a little with one of her own was just too much to bear. Now she wondered what she'd thought all the fuss was about. But then, she hadn't birthed these two—maybe that was it.

"When we get home, after I get you all settled, I have to go to the compound. It's my turn to train the Protectors." Jenny asked Valyn what it was he was teaching them. "Mostly it's the things that people say that make no sense to someone who might take what they say literally. Say, 'shut your mouth'—you don't mean for them to actually do that, but it's something that they might not know. Another one, and this one tripped me up once, is 'talk to the hand.' When I did that, the person took offense, like I was making fun of them."

"That's makes perfect sense to me. I can see where things like that would mess someone up that hasn't been here long. Even people from other countries have a bit of difficulty in figuring out what we're talking about." He said it was much the same way. "I've been put on medical leave for the time being. I was astonished to find out that they were paying me. Did you know that?"

"I think it might have been mentioned. Boss said that you were worth every penny of it too." She huffed, something that she had picked up from Janie. "You do that well. Not as well as Janie, but you're getting there. Does that mean you're displeased?"

"Sort of. But I guess it's all right. I'm going to put the money in the bank for the boys. You know, for school trips or something." He pointed out to her that they had plenty of money, she should use it for herself. "I am. This is what I want to do. Make them very happy that they're with us."

Davy was asleep when they arrived at the house. Valyn carried him into the house and she helped Connor. He was doing much better, she'd been told, better than they had expected. She was glad. It would be a long time before she was comfortable traveling that way again.

The man that had hit their car wasn't intoxicated; he had been simply driving too fast in the icy weather and had lost control of his car. And when he'd hit them, it had caused a chain reaction of other cars hitting them as well as each other. Most of the other people had been able to walk away from the accident, but there were others that were still recovering. It would be a long while, she thought, before it was all sorted out.

"Can I just lay down, Mom?" She got a little choked up whenever he called her that, so she was only able to nod. "I'm really tired, and I hurt a little. I should have taken that pill before we left like the doctor said to. I just want to take one now and go to sleep."

"All right. But Davy will be in the bed with you. Are

you sure you don't want to rest in the other room for now? I'd hate for him to roll over on you." He nodded, nearly crying by the time they got up the flight of stairs. "Come on now, buddy. Let's get you something for the pain and get you in bed."

He was asleep before she left him. Connor looked so tiny in the big bed, and she wanted to crawl in there with him, just to make sure he was safe. Going into the other bedroom, she saw that Davy was still asleep, and she whispered to Valyn what she'd done with Connor.

"You going to be all right being nursemaid to two little boys?" He was joking with her and she smacked him on the arm. Making their way out of the room, he pulled her to him and kissed her. "I should go. There is a lot going on over at the compound, and I'd hate to leave them hanging again. I haven't been there since the accident."

"Go. The sooner you get there and get done, the sooner you can come back to us. I'm going to ask Janie if she can just make me something light for lunch, then we'll all eat dinner together if they're feeling up to it." He said that was a splendid idea. "Thanks. I have them once in a while."

He swatted her ass as he went by her. She loved that man so much she wondered what she'd do without him in her life. Or the boys. Checking on them once more, she went down to the kitchen to talk to Janie. She could tell that something had upset her and sat down to talk to her.

"When I was coming over here before you got home, I thought I saw someone or something out by the garage. I wasn't sure that I had, but there were footprints in the snow." She asked her what this person looked like. "Nasty.

I don't know why that comes to mind, but that's what it looked like. I couldn't tell if it was a man or a woman, but they were lurking about the house. I could tell too because of the prints again."

"Did you ask Bonner if he saw anyone?" She said that he'd not seen anyone, but he was able to see some tracks inside the yard by the trees. "We'll have to make sure that the house is locked up tight."

Her mother was the first thing that popped into her head. She had a good idea that she had come to get money from her too. Margo Bash had called her a few days ago, telling her that her mom had camped out on her couch for a few weeks, and that she was headed toward her.

"Honey, you'd better take care that you don't get too close to her. She's not bathed in I don't know how long. And the only way they will be able to do anything to that nasty mop of hair she has is to cut it down to her head and be done with it." Jenny thanked her and told her that she'd be all right now. "You take care. I'm so glad that you've gotten yourself on a good footing. You should be very proud of yourself."

"I am. And thank you again."

Margo had been the only person from her past that she had talked to. Just after she'd gotten her first good paying job, Margo had reached out to her, sending her a card and telling her who she was. And that she'd not had any contact with her mom in some time. And since then, they'd been talking every week or so, just to catch up on things. They never talked about her mother again after that first conversation.

Now there was someone on the property and she was afraid it was her, but not that she was afraid of her. It's just that she didn't want her coming around. There was only ever one thing on her mind, and that was Jenny giving her money. And if not money, then something that she could sell for some. Jenny wasn't going to do that, not ever again.

After her mom had hit her across the face and left her on the side of the road, Jenny had had to find her own way in the world. It had been rough too. She'd been almost nine then, and had nothing but the clothing that she had on. It took her nearly two weeks to find her a place that felt safe, and longer still to figure out that her mom wasn't coming back for her. Going to the place that she'd left her would only make her cry because she was alone.

She'd found herself a couple, an elderly couple, that took her in. Jenny had helped them around the house, making sure that the house was clean and the trash was taken out. And in return, they kept her fed and with a bed to sleep in at night. After four years of helping each other, one morning the mister didn't wake up. They'd had to bury him in the beautiful cemetery that was close by. The missus had sat at the table, just staring out at nothing for a week before she'd gone to bed and never woke up either. The note she left Jenny, with cash inside, was all she had in the world.

She'd told her to go out and conquer the world. The two hundred dollars had helped a little, but not enough to conquer much more than getting her a place to stay. Jenny had always been tall for her age, and it had helped her land a job as a dishwasher in the same restaurant that she'd been nearly killed in.

When everything went to shit after the credit card scandal, she'd gone back to see if she could get a job and Jimmy had hired her on the spot. She'd been working there for a year or so when a man came in determined to kill them all.

"Miss?" She looked at Janie, who was staring at her as if she'd been saying her name for a while now. "Are you all right? You look like you've been through the ringer a few times."

"I was just thinking of my life before Valyn. I can't believe how much things have changed for me. And now I have kids." Janie told her that she was lucky indeed. "Yes, I do believe that I am."

Jenny spent the rest of the afternoon playing and hanging out with the boys. They'd woken from their nap and joined her in the living room and watched a movie. They had also pulled out some board games that she had no idea where they'd come from and had fun with that. As casually as she could, she told them about the person on the property.

"I don't know who it is, but I want you to stay indoors for a few days. This person might only be some homeless person looking for some food, but we don't know that right now." Davy asked if they needed a gun. "No, I don't think we need to have a gun, but you keep an eye out for the person, all right?"

"I'll protect you, Mom." She thanked him, and he sat in her lap. Connor was concentrating on something, and she asked him if he was all right.

"Yes. I just don't want you to be hurt again. They might be coming here to rob you or something. And that would be just terrible." She agreed with him on that, but did tell him that Bonner was at the gate. "He is, but that's a far way away. He might not make it here in time. I think that me and Davy, we'll keep an eye on things until Dad gets back. That way he won't come here and we're all upset because things got taken from him."

"I thank you for being so brave for me." She started to tell them that she had it under control when she looked at their little faces. They needed to do this for her. And she was going to let them. "I feel so much better that you guys are here with me. I really do."

The rest of the afternoon was spent the same way as before. Only now one or both of them would go to the windows and doors on the first level and look around. Neither one acted like they were afraid of what might be skulking out there, and that really did make her feel safe.

But Jenny knew that her mom was out there someplace, and she was going to cause all kinds of trouble for her. And the kids and Valyn would be drawn in with her. Jenny thought about giving her money, that was all she ever really wanted anyway. But that would be a never-ending thing. Her mom would suck them dry just because she could.

Well, not this time. She was going to stand up to her and make her see that she wasn't that eight-year-old that she'd left by the side of the road. She was a person of worth. Her mother was going to see a different person when she came here with her greasy paw out.

CHAPTER 12

Valyn was just finishing up putting the papers away when all the other Mystics came in the room with him. At first he thought that something had happened to his family, but Agon was quick to tell him that they were all fine. When he was asked to have a seat, he told them to just tell him.

"We know that the mother is on your land." He did sit then, and then stood up to leave. "She's doing nothing at the moment, but she's been around the house. Looking in windows and trying to get into the garage."

"How do you know that?" He was handed a small computer and was told to hit play. "Where did you get this from? It's my house."

"Yes. We've had cameras put up all over the compound, as well as at the houses of each of us. I meant to tell you earlier, but you had the boys then the accident. It didn't seem the right time to tell you we were watching you." Valyn thought of all the things they'd been doing in the hot

175

tub and looked at Agon. He cleared his throat and spoke again. "We're not watching you every moment, Valyn. I swear we aren't."

Watching the recording of his house, he saw the person moving up the drive then around the house. He couldn't tell who it was or even if it was a male or female. Then she turned and seemed to look right at the camera for a few moments. Valyn had never seen Jennifer's mom, and asked them how they knew it was her.

"Facial recognition program. It took it a while to figure her out too. The hair and how much weight she's lost was making it more difficult. But once we figured out who it might be, we did some searching and found out that she'd been on her way here." He asked Galin how he knew that part. "She hitched a right with a trucker as far as the town's limits. His Protector was helpful in verifying it was the same woman. He also told us that she stank. Not that he could smell her, but apparently the driver had to ride with his windows open for fifty miles before he could roll them back up. He complained about the smell for hours."

"So this is her, wandering around the property looking for Jennifer. Did she hurt Bonner or anyone else that is there?" Riss told him that she'd snuck by him when they'd left to pick up the boys from the hospital. "Do you think that she'll break in? Or just go to the door like she hasn't done anything wrong?"

None of them answered him and he stood up again. Riss started talking and telling them what they thought might happen. Pretty much what he'd said. She'd come right up to the door and knock. And she'd more than likely demand money from Jennifer.

"And failing that, she'll go to you for it. She figures, according to her Protector, that you'll be an easy target because you won't want your name slandered all over the place." Valyn told Galin that he didn't care about that, so long as his family was safe. "You know that, and I know that, but she has no idea what she's dealing with."

"Jennifer will need to be told." Arryn said that he thought she might already know. "How? Did she already go to the house?"

"Not yet, no. But Janie, your cook, noticed the extra footprints in the snow. She told Jenny as soon as she came into your house. And if Jenny is as smart as we know that she is, she's already warned the boys to stay inside and is preparing for a battle. So to speak." He asked Riss how he knew that. "Because, like I said, your Jenny is a smart girl."

All kinds of things ran through his mind. He wanted to go there now, but they were telling him the plan. Not that he was paying very good attention to it—he was more focused on his wife and sons. When Galin said his name, he looked at him.

"You zoned out." Valyn told him he was worried about his family. "As you should be. But we're taking precautions as well. There are extra people around the house. And when you leave here, we're going to go with you. A stronger force, I guess you could call us."

Telling him the plan again, they headed to their cars. Valyn reached out to Jennifer to see if she was all right. He smiled when she told him that the boys were protecting her from the evil woman.

So you know that it's her that's out there. Jennifer told him she wasn't positive, but was close enough to it. *The rest of the guys are coming over to hang out until we figure out what she wants.*

Money. It's always money. But I do appreciate the extra muscle around too. She was quiet for a bit and he asked her if she was all right. *Yes. I just hate that she's showing up right now. I wish never, but we're just getting things around here settled, and she's going to mess it all up. I know her.*

She might try, but we'll beat her. Even if we have to have her arrested for trespassing. She told him that wouldn't keep her from coming back. *No, but it will slow her down a little. How are you guys feeling? Do I need to bring home extra food for us all?*

No, I've told Janie how many for dinner and she's thrilled. I swear, this woman loves to cook for us. He laughed when she did. *I'll call the others in — might as well have a nice reunion while we're at it. The women and the babies.*

He felt better just talking to her. Valyn didn't know what this woman would want from them, but she'd most assuredly get more than she'd bargained for.

He was searching the grounds as he drove up the drive. And while he'd not seen anything out of the ordinary, just knowing that someone was out there gave him the creeps. Valyn got out of the car just as the rest of them pulled in the drive. They were a big group; maybe this would keep her away.

The entire family — because that was what he considered the others that he worked with — was very quiet, and tried not to tower over the boys. Davy wasn't nearly as timid as

Connor was, but after a little while, when he realized that no one was going to hurt him, Connor came around too. Davy asked if they all had wings.

"We do, young man. And you know not to tell anyone, don't you?" He told Riss that he'd never tell anyone about them. "I'm glad to hear that. It would be terrible if someone came here and tried to take us away. And they might hurt the babies or the other women while they were about it."

"I'm going to keep my mom safe too. If you wanna help, that's all right. But just don't get in my way. I might hurt you accidently." Riss nodded at him, just as straight faced as he could. Then when Davy went to check on the little ones, Riss laughed, as did the rest of them.

"You have yourself quite the dragon slayer, Jenny. I do believe if I were your mother, I'd be worried about that one." Jenny thanked Riss and told him that they'd been protecting her all day. "Good — as it should be with young men. They're good boys, as I'm sure you know. And lucky to have you as a parent."

"No, I'm the lucky one. To have such wonderful friends, a great husband, and two of the best little boys. There isn't anything other than for my mom to go away that I want or need."

Riss hugged her, then the others did as well.

Valyn considered himself to be very lucky too. To have all that he had, and all the wonder and magic that came with having a family. He looked out the window in the living room, just to gather his emotions again, and he saw her. She looked much worse in real life than she had in the pictures. And nasty didn't even begin to cover what she

179

looked like

"She's coming." They all looked where he was looking. "I want to know what you want to do, Jennifer. Whatever you wish is the way it will happen. Unless, of course, she tries to hurt any of you."

"She won't get a chance." Jennifer went to the door and opened it before her mother could knock or ring the bell. "Hello, Mother. What rock have you crawled out from under? Wherever it was, I suggest you go back there and leave me alone."

Valyn stood behind Jennifer and put his hands on her shoulders. He could feel the tension and the anger radiating from her. He wanted to pull Jennifer away and handle this for her, but he knew that it wouldn't end there or solve anything. He just let her do the talking.

"What a way to speak to me. You do remember that I'm your mother, don't you? That's no way to treat me." She didn't speak to her mother, and when she blocked her from coming in the house, Beth looked upset. "You're not even going to invite me in? It's cold out here, Jenny. Let me get in there and we talk about stuff."

"I'm not going to give you anything. No money, no shelter, nor am I going to allow you to hurt me again." Beth looked at him, and he could see that this woman would never give up on what she'd had decided was hers. "I don't have any idea how you found me, nor why you'd even care to. I'm finished with you, and you know the reason why. You would suck me dry if you could, then still be pissed off because there wasn't more for you. But this is how you left a young kid by the side of the road when you wanted a fuck buddy."

"My God, how long are you going to hold that against me? So what? I left you by the road while I pursued some of the things that I deserved. Having you hanging around was cramping my style." Jennifer asked her if this was supposed to be her style. "I've run into a bit of hard luck, which you're going to help me out of."

"No, I'm not." She started to close the door in her face, but Beth stuck her boot in the door before she could. "Go away."

"I want you to give me some money. It's the least you can do after all I did for you." Jennifer asked her what that might have been. "Well, you're not dead, for one thing. What if I told you that I kept you from being raped by the men I had around? They would have paid good money to have you."

"I don't believe you. First of all, you would have sold me off for the first flashy thing that they waved in front of you. Secondly, you were too busy getting stoned to pay any attention to anyone but yourself." Beth tried her best to get in the door again, but Jennifer had her blocked well. "You're not welcome here. Not now, not ever. You gave up any rights to demand things from me the moment you pulled away from your eight-year-old daughter."

Beth looked at him. "You will hand over some cash, won't you, big guy? I mean, my rude assed daughter here didn't even introduce us. I'm Beth Hale. And you are...?"

"Valyn Slayer. And these are our sons, Connor and Davy Slayer." The boys were right behind them, and he wanted her to know that Jennifer had a life here that did not include her. "My wife has asked you to leave, and I believe it is past time for you to do so."

"You have kids? Holy shit, Jenny, you got yourself some snot nosed kids? Never would have thought that—"

"You're a rude person and I don't like you." Davy pushed his way in front of Jennifer, and before Valyn could reach for him to get him out of harm's way, Connor had joined him. "We don't want you here, nasty lady. Now, my mom and dad told you to go away, and you'd better, or I'm calling up someone to make you."

Connor doubled up his fist and watched Beth. When she got down to their level, both of them put their hands over their mouth and nose. Even from where he was, Valyn could tell that she'd not bathed in a very long time, and that she had a smell that he could only call doped.

"You're my grandkids. Holy shit, she's made me a grandma. I'm not nearly old enough to be that to you brats."

Connor popped his good fist right into her mouth, and when she went tumbling back onto the porch, Davy sat over top of her and held her down. Valyn wasn't sure if he should be impressed or afraid for the boys.

"You're not our grandma. And we don't want you to be even if you wanted to be." Beth struggled, but apparently Davy wasn't budging as Connor spoke. "I had my uncle call the police, and I'm going to hold you here until they come. I'm not going to let you hurt any of us. Do you understand?"

"I understand that as soon as I get up from here, I'm going to snap your little neck like a twig. Get off me, you rotten piece of flesh." Valyn heard the police coming as Beth tried to get up again. "I swear to Christ, you're going to get the shit knocked out of you, see if you don't."

Connor didn't engage with her again, and Davy just kept bouncing up and down on her until she lay still. No one moved to help him, but Davy and the two of them kept her contained until the police were up on the porch.

"Hello, Valyn, Jenny. Riss called us in. Told us to come and take out the trash." Someone behind him laughed. "She sure is going to smell up the jail and the car, but what can you do? Come on, Ms. Hale, I'm hauling you in for trespassing."

She screamed all the way to the cruiser. Jennifer pulled the boys in the house and shut the door. When she turned to him, he could see tears in her eyes and pulled her to him. But he realized a minute later that she was laughing. He joined her. There wasn't anything funny about any of this, yet it felt good to do it.

~*~

Beth didn't know how she'd gotten arrested and brought to jail, but she was gonna sure make her daughter pay for this. She didn't know how or when, but she'd get back at her. And to think, she'd went and made her a fucking grandma.

Pacing the cell back and forth, Beth tried her best to stop shaking. It was getting bad, she thought. The need for a hit was making her skin crawl. Looking up when someone said her name, the water from a hose hit her square in her bloodied lip.

"What the fuck are you doing? Stop that right now."

The water pressure was so strong that it was tearing at her clothing. Her hair was hanging down on her face, and she could smell how bad it had gotten. "Stop. You can't do this to me. I have rights."

"So do we in not having to smell you anymore. Even the other prisoners are willing to go to prison to get away from you." The water kept coming at her, like it was a fucking fire hose or something. When they turned it off, she was tossed a bar of soap and a big rag. "Wash yourself, or we'll come in there and do it for you. And if you have one lice on your body, someone is going to cut that nasty shit off your head."

"You are going to be in so much trouble when I get to talk to my daughter." The cop asked her who she thought this idea came from. "You're kidding me. She'd not tell you to use a hose on me like that."

Beth washed herself with the rag she'd been given, and wasn't too terribly shocked when it came away nearly black. Picking up the soap, Beth was shaking for an entirely different reason now. It was fucking cold, and she was nearly naked and soaking wet.

They kept it up for at least an hour. She'd wash off and they'd hit her with the hose again. When one of them came into the cell with a pair of scissors, Beth backed up and told them to get away.

"You either let me check your head out, or I let these others hold you down while they do. And let me tell you, bothering the Slayers like you did? Ain't a one of us that won't want to hurt you in some way. That Ms. Jenny? She held my momma's hand while she was dying. I was coming to her, but Jenny, she stood in my place until I was able to get there." She clipped those scissors together two times, like she was going to use them despite what she wanted. "Now, we're going to have us a looksee."

Beth told her that Jenny was a tramp, that she was a whore and a drug addict. Anything that she could think of, she spewed it out to these people to make them see reason. But she still came at her, clipping the scissors over and over.

She knew that she had head lice. Hell, the way she was always laying around in somebody else's roll, it was small wonder she didn't have more than that. As she was pulled to the floor to have her hair cut off, she could see the little suckers running for cover. Christ, this was just about as bad as it had ever been for her.

After they'd cut all her hair off and put it in a big red bag that said *bio hazard* on it, she was hosed down again. Washing her head actually felt good after having the shit weighing her down all the time. When she was done, or at least they were satisfied, they gave her a towel, and when she finished they put it right in there with her hair and clothes.

The orange clothing that she was given after being put in a different cell wasn't soft, but it was clean. They didn't have bras or panties for her, so she had to go commando. Not that she cared, Beth didn't wear those things much anyway. Sitting on the bed, after all the adrenaline was wearing off, she was really hard up for a hit of something. Beth thought she was dying.

She saw a man come in when she was at her peak of hurting. Her belly felt like it was crawling up behind her throat. Her skin, even though it was cleaner than it had been in longer than she could remember, felt like it was shrinking around her. Then it would itch like it had when she'd gotten into some poison ivy some time back.

There was a pinch to her arm and then she was floating. It wasn't enough, but it took the edge off. Reaching for the person she was getting high with, she realized that her hands were chained up, like they were having them some kinky sex or something. She told him that she needed more.

"No, you're not going to get any more than that until you're dried out." The man wasn't making any sense and she told him that. "You're in jail, Ms. Hale, and you have been for four days. I'm here to help you out and to wean you off the drugs. Slowly. I would imagine that you've been taking them since you learned how."

"You know it. But why do you hold back on a girl? Come on, give me another hit. I won't tell anybody." He didn't even crack a smile at her. "I'm going to be hurting here soon. Why don't you leave it here with me and I'll not use it all at once? You can trust me."

"I wouldn't trust you with a sheet of paper right now. Are you listening to me?" She nodded. "My name is Doctor Phillips. I'm in this cell with Elizabeth Hale, fifty-year-old woman with a drug addiction. She's been brought in on trespassing charges as well as breaking and entering, malicious conduct, and defacing a person's home."

"Not right. My lovely daughter, the bitch, wouldn't let me in the house, so I didn't break in at all." He told her he was referring to the Miller home. "Who the fuck are the Millers? I didn't break into their house. Don't you think I'd

186

have more money on me had I done that?"

"You apparently slept in their garage and defaced the floor, as well as a few other items. That's where the B&E comes in." She told him how they'd left the door wide open. "And did they invite you in? Ask you to sleep on the floor, using the dog's blankets? No, they didn't. And by the way, the dog wouldn't even sleep on those blankets again. And he drinks out of commodes."

"Maybe we can work something out. I'm not made for jail time. I'm a free spirit, and I can't be cooped up in this cell for very long." He told her to get used to it. "What do you mean, get used to it? What the hell else are you making up to charge me for?"

"There are several warrants out for your immediate arrest in Georgia, Florida, and New Mexico. And those are only the states that came forward when we put out that you'd been caught. You've been really busy, haven't you?" She smiled, thinking that he was at least seeing her side of things. "Bank robbery. Liquor store robbery, and also another charge of malicious conduct. You also sold some drugs to an undercover officer, then ran away when things got too hot. Driving without a license, DWI...the list goes on and on, but I'm sure you know that."

"You can't pin that all on me. I know, what if I give you other names? Some of the people who helped me. That'll get me a lower sentence, won't it? If nothing else, it should get me a few freebie hits from whatever you gave me before." He told her no; just like that, no. "Come on. I need it. I'm going crazy here too. Let me at least talk to my daughter. She can be made to help me out."

"That's not going to happen either, I'm afraid. She said that she wanted absolutely nothing to do with you and whatever trouble you might be in."

Angry now, Beth tried to pull away from the cuffs that held her to the bed. Cursing at him and her daughter, she got a headache from screaming.

When she calmed down enough to think, she was alone in the cell. No less chained up, but she was at least on a bed. She had to talk to Jenny. There wasn't any way that she'd think that leaving her in here was going to make her leave. Especially since she'd put her in here in the first place.

Laying on her back, thinking hard on how to get out of this mess she was in, all she could come up with was Jenny coming down here and bailing her out. Sure, they'd had their differences, but this was some serious shit going on here. She might have to go to prison for some of the shit that she'd done. But how to tell Jenny that when she'd not even speak to her.

Dinner was brought to her. Opening up the covered lids, she could only stare at the food there. There was roast beef over noodles and green beans, as well as a roll and butter. A piece of peach pie for dessert, and a cup of strong black coffee along with a can of pop. *Hell,* she thought, *I might just stay here if they're going to feed me like this every day.*

When the guard came in she was told not to move, or they'd hurt her again. When he unlocked her right wrist, she had a moment there when she thought that she could overpower him and get away. But he looked at her and she felt her power shrivel up like a dried-up flower.

"Do it and you'll never see the light of day again. I will not be fucked with, you hear me?" She nodded. "Good. Now eat your dinner before it gets cold. Then I'll be back to lock you back up."

"Why can't I just have one of my arms locked up? Come on, nobody will know." He just kept going. "I can make it worth your while if you do. I'm good at giving head."

He stopped and looked at her. Licking her lips, she was thinking that he was surely interested when he shuddered and left her sitting there. Fucking bastard—he was more than likely one of those queers. She ate her dinner and was cuffed back up after the tray was taken away. There was no hope for it right now, she was going to be stuck here for a while. At least until she could convince Jenny that she was going to help her.

CHAPTER 13

Jenny was set to go. She was going to drop off the boys at the private school that they were going to, then she had a couple of things to do on her own. Connor was excited but scared. The other school and the teachers there had done that to him. She was going to talk to them today — one thing on her list.

Davy was purely excited to be going to the new school. He'd already got to meet his teacher and was given a list of things that he'd need for his class. They were starting so late in the year that she worried about them falling behind, but they both had been tested and scored high marks on it.

When she pulled up in front of the school, Davy leaped out, but Connor sat there.

"What if they heard about us?" She told him that they had. "Who told them that we were dirty boys? Did you?"

"No. The only thing they know about you is the praise that Valyn and I gave you both and the teachers who saw your test scores. You did well." He didn't move. "You do know that no one will know you here. And that means you can start fresh. You can be Connor Slayer, brilliant boy who wears very nice clothes."

"Maybe someone told them about me when they got my records." She told him she was going to get them herself and bring them to the school. "Ms. Cochran didn't talk to them?"

"No, and she won't, either." She wanted to tell him that she was going to the school to take care of both the boys' teachers, as well as the principal. "You go in and have a good day, and myself or Valyn will be here to pick you up. All right?"

"Yes, all right. But if someone makes fun of me, I'm going to call you and have you come and get me. I can't stand to be called names anymore." She kissed him on the cheek and told him that she was only a phone call away. "I love you, Mom. Thank you for being the best mom in the world."

When he got out of the car and ran up the steps, she sat there for a few minutes gathering herself together. He loved her. And he'd called her the best mom in the world. Jenny thought that she could live on that for the rest of her life.

Driving to the other school was a little scary for her. The accident had made her a nervous wreck, and she wasn't all that sure at driving anyway. By the time she pulled into the parking lot, her hands were sweaty and they hurt when she pulled them off the steering wheel.

She had called the school board yesterday and set this up. Jenny had told them who she was, who her boys were, and the circumstances of why she had them. Not the whole of it, but enough for them to know that she wasn't happy with the way things had been for them.

One member of the board was going to meet her here at eleven, and it was just shy of that now. Going up to the front door, she was surprised to find the security guard standing at the front counter talking to the woman there. No sign of anyone watching who came and went. The woman from the school board, Shelly Pace, was just behind her and asked him what he was doing.

"Nothing. I was just having a conversation with Mary here. Did you know that she took first prize in the baking contest over the weekend? She brought me in some of it." Shelly told him he was to be at the door at all times. "Nothing ever happens around here, anyway. It's sort of boring to just stand there."

Shelly looked at Jenny and said nothing. When they were both in the office of the principle, she could smell beer. Looking around while no one was there but the two of them, Shelly not only found one of the empty cans in the trash can, but four more in her little fridge near the filing cabinets.

They were both seated when Mrs. Cochran came in the room, ten minutes late. Mrs. Dufrene, also late, came in a bit later. They seemed to not know who Shelly was, and Jenny didn't introduce them to her.

"I'm here to get a transcript for Connor and Davy Bass." The principle seemed stunned by the request and asked her why. "They've been enrolled in a different school, and they need them. Can I get them and any other paperwork

193

they might need?"

"Sure. I have to tell you, I'm glad that they're no longer here." Shelly asked her why. "Well, they were dirty and smelled. They never had the money for fees and such, and don't get me started on how many times they were turned away from the lunch counter. The other kids didn't want to play with them, and we didn't encourage it either. I mean, who wants their kids associating with trash like that?"

"They're my sons now." The teacher and the principal both looked at her and started laughing. "And why do you think that's the least bit funny?"

"You and those kids together. I mean, beg my pardon, but you look like you have some money. Why would you want those children next to you? They probably have head lice too." Jenny started to stand up but was held down by Shelly. "They rarely had any food either, and we had to cut them off when there wasn't any money coming in for it after the first couple of weeks they started here."

"So you let them starve?" Mrs. Cochran shrugged and looked in the file cabinet. "Did you happen to find out why there was no money coming in? Or why they were battered and bruised up? I saw one of their school photos, and Davy had a black eye and Connor a busted lip, as well as blood on his face. Why were they hurt like that, do you know?"

"I don't know who you think you are, but we don't have time to go inspect every kid that comes in here. There are two hundred and ten students in this school. I have to spend my time making sure that there is enough funding to go around for deadbeat kids like those. The teachers should be responsible for that." She handed her the transcripts. "I think it's about time you both leave. I have a school to run, and I don't have time to sit here and be taken apart by two women that don't have the sense to get out of the rain."

"Mrs. Cochran, Mrs. Dufrene, you're both fired. I'm the new school director, and I'm appalled at what I've witnessed here in the last half hour." They both started talking at once. "Silence."

The room got so quiet that she could hear the guard out front talking to Mary again. This would not bode well for him either, Jenny thought. When Shelly stood up, so did she. And when she turned to her, she had a very sad smile on her face.

"I'm so grateful for you calling us on this. Had you not, I shudder to think how much longer this would have gone on. And the way they were speaking about those children, any child like that, they should be ashamed of themselves." When she put out her hand, Jenny took it and thanked her. "No, it's us that will be thanking you for this. I've got this now. You go on and get your sons an ice cream when they get home. Lord knows they deserve it."

Jenny decided to head over to the compound to tell Valyn what had happened. When she got there they were going through drills and she sat back to watch. There was something so soothing about watching someone do simple tasks like exercising in the outdoors.

Others were working on speech, as well as common words that could trip someone up. Learning how to recognize money and the worth of each denomination. Writing a check out to pay for goods, even how to use a credit card and how to track how much was being spent.

These were things that she'd never thought of as something that people like these wouldn't know.

"They've been here for a very long time, yet never thought to learn any of the human ways. They just protected." Jenny asked Boss when he joined her if that was why so many of them were wanting to do something else. "I believe so. I have seen that they're better equipped at keeping an eye on their humans too. How to spot a scam, and when it's time to call the police."

"I was just thinking how it seems so unreal to me that they wouldn't have picked some of this up. But I guess, as you said, they were only there to protect." The two of them watched the field for a little while longer. "I had a productive day. But now that I think on it, I got at least two people fired today. I don't know if that was such a good thing to be happy about."

"You did what was right for the children, all of them coming and going through those classrooms. Think how much better at being around strangers your sons would be if they'd had the proper care, or someone to take the time to see what was going on. They might not have spent so many years in such an abusive home." She nodded and told him it was still difficult. "Yes, I know that as well. Sometimes it's harder to do the right thing than the one that isn't so smart. I heard that your mother came to see you all."

"She did. And now she's in jail. I had no idea she was wanted in other states. I mean, I guess I could have figured that out, but she really hasn't been all that good of a person." He didn't say anything, for which she was

196

grateful. "I'm going to go and see her today. I have a few things I'd like to clear the air with her about."

"You should do that. I'm to understand from a contact of mine that she will be moved to one of the states that she has a warrant in to have her day in court." Jenny said that she'd heard that as well. "I think you should take one of the other women with you. Not because you need protecting, but it would be nice to have someone there when she gets to spewing forth her belief about how you have mistreated her."

"Yes, well, she's been telling me that for a long time. And the fact that she left me beside the road, while she went on her fun, in her mind was saving me. I don't understand her. Or even people that treat their children this way." Again he said nothing, but she could see the pain in his eyes. "Are you getting enough rest? I mean, I know from Tholan that you never sleep. But you are taking a little time off now and then, aren't you?"

"I come here when I can get away. I wanted to talk to you about Valyn. I despaired of him falling in love with you. He had his heart hardened long ago." She said that he'd told her. "Did he tell you also that he would have nightmares for a very long time after that? Even before you came, I think they were still plaguing him. But he's been well since the two of you have been mates. I thank you for that."

"It was my pleasure, actually. I'm in love with him, and I don't think I could have been this loved by anyone else but him. And now we have children of our own. I love them to pieces too." He told her as it should be. "Who is next on your list of Mystics? I have an idea, but will you tell me who it is?"

"Tholan. I think he will be the hardest of all to convince this is the right thing for him to be doing. He has had his heart broken as well, but by his own deeds. He does not get out as much as I'd like for him to either. That is why he has so much trouble relating to the others." She said that she'd thought that he hated her for a while. "He doesn't know how to show that he likes someone. It's been...I was going to say that it isn't in his heart, but that's not right. It's his head that prevents him from being one of the greatest Protectors ever created."

"The woman that comes to him, she'll need to be very capable of kicking his butt but good." He laughed and she smiled. "You should do that more often—laugh, I mean. But Tholan, I'm not sure if he's had that particular emotion taken out of him at some point. He needs to laugh more too."

"I hope for the same thing daily." He nodded toward the field. "I do believe that they are ready for their lunch. You go and tell Valyn about your visit, and I will work on what I have in store for our Tholan. And please don't tell him. It'll be more fun if he is unaware until it's too late."

"I won't tell anyone."

He nodded and told her goodbye just as Valyn joined her. After the two men shook hands, Boss disappeared and she and Valyn went to the large dining area. She couldn't wait to watch Tholan come to terms with someone to love him.

~*~

Kala had jumped at the chance to go with Jenny to see her mom. The woman should have been horsewhipped a long time ago for what she'd done to her child. But, if she was honest about things, Jenny might not have turned out so nice had she been able to hang out with her mother and been a part of her deeds.

"She doesn't like me." Kala stared at her before bursting out laughing. "Yes, well, I guess you would know that. I think that everyone does."

"Yes, I heard that one of your sons punched her in the mouth. I wish I could have seen that. It must have been a sight. I do hope you sanitized his hands when she was taken away." This time Jenny laughed. "They're coming along nicely, the boys are. It's hard for me to believe that only a week ago they were terrified of everyone and wouldn't allow anyone to touch them."

"I know. But they were still healing from some of the wounds that had been inflicted on them. And then the accident too. Every time I close my eyes, I can still see Connor attached to all those machines to help him breathe." Kala said that she might not have driven again. "I didn't want to, but Valyn said that if I didn't right away, then I never would. He assured me over and over that it was an accident and those happen to everyone."

"He's too smart for his own good, that one is." They were at the jail when Kala turned to Jenny. "Why are you doing this? Seeing your mom, I mean. You know that whatever she says to you, it's either going to be a lie or something that she wants to hurt you with. I don't want you hurting that way again."

"Neither do I, but I'm doing this for me, not her. I need for her to know that this is over, there will not be any more visits, and I'm not going to give her any money. I don't know that it will work, but that's the plan." Kala got out of the car when Jenny did. "Besides, I've heard that she's been bathed, and her hair fixed. While I'm not sure what that would entail—it was all nasty if you ask me—but she might be better to stand next to now."

"I heard that she was foul smelling. Hopefully they get her to take a shower every day, or it won't be as pleasant at the next place she goes. Where is that, by the way?" Jenny told her that the larger crime that she had committed was in Georgia. She'd go there first. "What was that one, if you don't mind me asking?"

"Armed robbery, and a hit on a liquor store too. She had people with her, and I guess if she gives them up, it will lessen her sentence. But when I spoke to Renie about it, she said that with all the other charges she has against her, she won't be getting out for a very long time, if ever." Kala knew that she'd serve each sentence consecutively for each state she was tried in. "On a more pleasant note, the boys both tested higher than their grade level. Connor is a whiz at math, and one of the teachers is going to have one of the high school teachers come over twice a week to challenge him with harder things than he will get in second grade."

They were in the jail now, and one of the officers was leading them back to the cells. He was telling them not to be too surprised by her appearance. The hair had to come off, as it was full of lice and other things. Also, while she was clean, she still had a strong odor about her.

Kala watched Jenny brace herself to walk down the short hall to her mom's cell. It was the last one in the row of cells, and if she wanted to, they could leave and Beth would never know they were there. But Kala was there for support, not to talk her out of seeing her. Jenny was a lot stronger than she was. Kala would have just left Beth to rot her ass in jail for the rest of her life.

Their footsteps seemed to be loud in the otherwise silent hall. She thought it odd that all the other inmates were as quiet as church mice. Looking in a couple of the cells, she noticed that no one was looking at them after the first glance. Kala was glad for that. She didn't want them trying to talk to them today.

"Mother." Kala looked at the woman in the cell when Jenny called out to her. "Mother, I've come to tell you a few things."

"I don't give a holy rat's patootie what you have to say to me. So, fuck the hell off if you're not here to bail me out or give me some cash so I can pay these fuckers off to let me slide on by them."

Kala watched Beth. She looked all of her fifty years and more so. With her hair gone she looked thinner, gaunter than she imagined she'd be. There were sores all over her face and arms, and it looked like she'd been scratching at them until they were bloodied. Her lips were dry, and it looked to her like they were peeling off. Then her smell hit her.

"Holy crap, you still smell like the back end of a horse's ass." Jenny laughed. Beth, however, didn't think it was the least bit funny, and came at her, screaming. There wasn't any way that she could touch her, but Kala still backed away from her. "You need to back up, woman. Otherwise I'm going to be sick all over you."

Beth didn't move, but she didn't try and grab her again. Jenny just stared at her, and Beth seemed more interested in her dirty nails than her only child. When Jenny said her name this time, forgoing calling the woman "Mother" anymore, that finally got her attention.

"What the hell do you want, Jennifer? I guess that's what you go by now. That fucking shit, your husband, calls you that. Are you all formal now that you married above your paygrade?" Jenny asked her what that was supposed to mean. "You're nothing but white trash and always will be. Your father could be any one of a million men that I slept with, and none of them were very smart to begin with. Hell, for all I know, you could be some foreigner's kid. That would be just dandy, don't you think?"

"I couldn't care less how I was conceived. And for the record, I knew you were a whore before you left me by the road that day." Jenny smiled at her and Kala looked at Beth. Whatever Jenny said next, it was going to be impressive. "I found your mother and father. We're going to have dinner next week when they come to town to meet my sons."

"You lie. They're both dead." Jenny just stood there. "What the fuck are you going to them for? You got enough money. Are you hoping that they'll leave their long-lost granddaughter all that they have? They won't. Because they hate me that much."

"Yes, they do. And you might be happy or not, I don't

202

care, to know that you have a sister and a brother. Your parents adopted them when you left home." Beth called her a liar again. "No, I have no reason to lie to you, as you have me all of your life."

"So the fuck what? You going to go home and cry on your pillow because your mommy treated you badly? Grow up. No one cares how I treated you, and I doubt very much that your husband knows all about you either. I give you six months. Wait, that won't work, will it? You already have kids older than that. Did he have to marry you, Jennifer? Is that the reason that you got such a rich fuck to marry you?"

"You can think whatever you want about myself and my family. But I came here to tell you that you're no longer going to be able to contact me. There will be no visits to you while you're in prison. No money for you to try and bribe someone to let you out. As of when I leave here, you no longer exist to me or my boys." Beth laughed, and Jenny took a step closer to the cell. "You might want to ask your doctor what sort of things you might have picked up with your habit of borrowing needles, Elizabeth. I think you only have about a year left anyway."

With that she turned and walked away. Kala stood there for several seconds, just watching Beth as she dealt with what Jenny had just told her. When Beth finally looked at her, she asked her if that was right. Did she really have that queer disease?

"You're a piece of work, aren't you? Christ, and to think that you birthed that wonderful human being. I want to personally thank you for leaving her beside the road that day. I can't even comprehend what was going through your mind when you did that, but I'm glad you did. She turned out to be a human being of worth, while you are nothing but a.... You know, I have no good name to call you. Everything I can think of pales in comparison to what you are." Beth told her if she came closer to the bars, she'd show her what sort of person she was. "Yes, a bitch to the very end. No, I think I'll go with my friend and laugh about the pitiful woman that we left here. You are a sick fuck, and I'm so glad that I got to be here when Jenny told you."

She walked away then. Beth was screaming at her to come back, that she wanted to know what Jenny was talking about. But she didn't even turn around. There wasn't any point in standing there talking to a woman like her. She was only out for herself, and Kala wanted no part of her madness.

Jenny was sitting on one of the benches outside the station house, holding her face up to the sunshine with her eyes closed. Kala wasn't sure that she realized she was there until she spoke to her.

"My grandparents were so happy to hear from me. They said that they had written Beth off years ago. And they'd not known that she had abandoned me." Kala asked her how she'd found them. "Boss helped me some, but Dusty did the rest of it. They're not going to see Beth. I don't think it would do them any good to be insulted or hurt by her. And she would, simply because she can."

"You're right about both of those. She isn't even close to being nice. She's like, mean times a million." Jenny looked at her with a smile. It was a good one too. "How about I call in the other troops and we have dinner in town? Just the women. It'll be fun, and I think you can use it."

"I could, and thanks, I like that idea. Valyn said that he was getting off early and picking up the boys. They'll love having manly time with him." Jenny stood up and hugged her. Kala asked her what that was for. "You gave me strength in there. I didn't get in the mud with her, so to speak. I let her say what she wanted, then I said my piece. I think that I'll rest better now knowing that she can no longer hurt me."

Kala thought it would be a long time before her friend rested easy. She would still have feelings about her mom, no matter what sort of person she was. As they drove to the restaurant in town, Kala wondered if her own children would be the same way. No, she'd not be someone they would hate. She'd love them forever.

EPILOGUE

Tholan looked over the rotation again. He had sent it to Michael, as he did every week to let him approve it. There had never been any changes before, and he was flabbergasted to find that he'd marked through a couple of the names and put Tholan's there. He couldn't be a Protector. He just couldn't. He went to find Michael to ask him about it.

"I've been thinking that it might do you some good to go out once in a while. You're always stuck in the office, and you're getting behind in some of the things that are going on this century. It will be fun for you." He shook his head, his heart going so fast that he was sure Michael could hear it. "I can partner you with someone if you would like. I know that it has been a very long time for you."

"You keep saying that. It's been a long while because I want it to be." Tholan let out a long breath as he tried to control his emotions. "I cannot go back and mess up again, Michael. You know what happened the last time I was there."

"I do. And I believe that everyone would think that you've more than paid for what you've done. You made a mistake; we all do, and you'll be fine." Tholan shook his head, his fear of screwing up making him ill. "Why don't you go and talk to the others? Riss and Galin, any of them, for a few pointers."

"No one has ever made the mistake I have. That woman wasn't to die, and I took her too soon." Michael said that he was aware of what happened. "What if I do it again? I might, you know."

"No, I don't believe that you'll ever make that mistake again. I have faith in you." Michael smiled at him. "You'll do fine, Tholan. As I said, it will be very good for you to get out again."

Tholan made his way back to his office. He was going to mess up again, and this time there wouldn't be any making up for it. This time he'd be cut asunder by Michael. There was no coming back from that. Michael's sword was made just for that.

He was sitting at his desk again, his head in his hands, when he felt someone in the room with him. It was Boss, and he hoped that he was there to tell him that Michael had made a mistake and that he'd not have to go. But he sat down and asked him if he was excited to be going out on a mission.

"No, I'm not at all excited. I'm terrified, if you wish the truth of the matter. Please tell me that you will reconsider this. I would rather watch a worm than to be with another human. And worms, you know as well as I, are very boring creatures. But I won't harm one of them should I make another mistake." Boss asked him if he would purposely harm a human. "Goodness no. I'd rather cut myself than to harm even a hair on someone's head. No, but I might make another mistake."

"You won't." Tholan asked him if he was willing to take the chance on him making one. "I am. I have more faith in you than I do anyone else, Tholan. But you're too sated in being here for so long. You need to stretch out your wings and be with humans for a while. It won't be so bad, and you might grow to like it."

"I don't even think that is possible." He wanted to sob, something that he'd not done in decades, not since he'd made the mistake. "I guess it's my fate to go there and be with a human."

"It is. And you will thank me for it when you are finished."

Boss stood up and so did he. There was no hope for it; in four days he'd be with a human for the rest of its life. Whatever was he going to do?

"Don't think on it too hard, my good man. You'll make yourself sick for nothing."

Tholan couldn't even work, he was so stressed about this. The computer was turned off, so there weren't any messages coming in for him to see to. He wished that he could convince someone that this was going to be a fatal mistake. Turning on his computer to try and work, he saw that not only were there no messages for him to look into, but there wasn't anything for him to do now that the schedule was taken care of.

When his shift was over, he made his way to his room. It was as stark as his office, no clutter around like the others had. Tholan supposed it wasn't actually clutter, but he didn't even have the first picture hanging on the wall, nor curtains over the massive window.

His bed had a mattress that he'd had for several years, now lumpy and flat in places. His blankets were a pale brown, not a bright color, and there were no rugs in his room to cover the cold floor. His closet was devoid of clothing, and he only had one pair of boots that he hadn't ever worn because he was saving them for when the ones he had on wore out.

"Oh, what am I to do?" He laid down on the lumpy mattress and stared up at the ceiling. Even the light in this room was a single bulb that didn't even have a cover over it. "What am I going to do with all the colors and fast-moving things when I get there? How many changes have I missed over the years that I will not know? The few times I have been there, I was only there but a moment or two, and that was too much. Being there for a lifetime will be like a prison sentence to me."

He knew that he was going a little too far with his woes, but he did not want to mess up again. That was the real issue. He hadn't yet forgiven himself for what he'd done. Tholan wasn't even sure that he ever would. Taking a life — it's what he'd done. And there was nothing anyone could have done about it.

Instead of going back to his computer, he pulled a book from the shelf and began to read it. If the others knew what sort of stories he read in his room, they would surely make fun of him.

Tholan loved a good romance story, the kind that some of the humans, he heard, called bodice rippers. It was an apt name, he thought, and pulled it open to the chapter he'd been reading last night before he'd gone to sleep.

It was a common story. The man saved the woman from some dastardly deed and ended up breaking her heart in some way. And before he was able to redeem himself with her, he had to walk through hoops. But it was worth it in the end. They lived happily ever after.

Tholan wasn't sure that was the reason he read the books that he did. The happily ever after part. He knew that he'd never have that sort of ending. He wasn't like the others, the ones that had found mates and could make them happy. Tholan had never been responsible for anyone but himself. Taking care of a woman would be difficult if the women he knew on the compound were any indication. They were frightful to him in the ways that they said and did what they wanted. He rolled to his side and laid the book on the floor.

Tholan knew that he wasn't a bad looking man. He was tall, like the others of his kind. He had a good smile when he had the occasion to use it, which hadn't been much in the last few decades. And his face was smooth when he wished it to be. Reading his books had alerted him to that. Women didn't care for scruffy.

Not that any woman would come to him. He would just be the man that he was forever. Tholan hated feeling sorry for himself, so he got up and shook off the mood. Looking around his room, the only one that he'd ever had, he wondered about adding a little to it.

He could go to the other plane and get himself a nice comforter. That would put him with the humans, and perhaps it wouldn't be as bad as he thought. Sitting down again, he tried to remember when he'd last seen one of the others, how they were dressed.

Standing when he had on a pair of blue jeans and a shirt, he thought about how he looked. Fashionable, yet not too standout-ish. Yes, he was ready to go. Now to get some money. He had plenty of that, and he'd be set.

Sitting on his bed, he thought this was one of the worst ideas he'd ever had. He didn't know why he felt that he could do this. Putting his book back on the shelf, he almost missed the cover on the next book in the series.

It was of a beautiful woman and a man, much like him, tall and dark haired. The woman wore a gun. She had on jeans and a T shirt that outlined her body so that there was no doubt that she was a woman. But it was what was in the background of the two of them together that drew his attention.

There was a dove in the tree, its feathers brilliantly white. The green around her made her seem all the more pretty. He could see no reason whatsoever why there was a dove there, nor how to explain how the snowy white feather was in her mouth.

Tholan put it away—he was being silly. He was sure that once he read the book, it would come abundantly clear why she was there. He just wasn't going to think about it now—he still had half of the other book to read. Yes, he wasn't going to think about it, and took himself to the little town they were all living in.

~*~

"Prisoner number four four eight, come to the front." PJ moved to where she'd been told. "Prisoner number four four eight, come with me."

She followed behind the man in front of her. PJ had been known as four four eight for so long, she sometimes had to remind herself that she was a real person with a real name. Parker Jane Brooks. Most of the time she had spent on the outside she'd been called by her initials. But she was going to take on a new life now, and she'd go by Parker.

Today she was being set free. After nine years, eleven months, and twenty-three days, she was going to be free. She didn't have a clue what she was supposed to do now, other than to abide by the rules and do nothing that would send her back. Not that she'd done anything anyway, but in order for her dad to live out his last days a free man, she'd taken the fall for him.

Parker Daniel Brooks had been the greatest man she knew. PD to his buddies, to her he was always Da. He'd died the second year she'd been in here, and she'd not been able to go to his funeral. And other than her attorney, telling her that she had inherited his estate, she'd not had a single visitor for the last seven years.

Being in the wrong place at the wrong time was an understatement. He wasn't there at all. The robbery of the little liquor store had come as a huge surprise to him, as well as her stepmother. But they had a witness that had said he was there, and that he'd held a gun on the owner until he was able to leave with all the money and a bottle of cheap wine.

First of all, Da didn't drink, cheap or otherwise. He didn't know how to hold a gun, much less fire one. And the fact that they had him running away was erroneous. Her da had been in a wheelchair for most of his adult life. But the eyewitnesses had pointed him out, even with him sitting in his chair. It was then that PJ knew that they were only arresting him to get the robbery off their yearend books.

So when it became evident that her da was being railroaded, she stepped up and confessed to it all. Any idiot within five miles of her knew that she looked nothing like her father, in weight or height. But the police and the prosecuting attorney had leapt on it like it was a lifeline. Parker had done this for him. And only him.

She was let out of the big mammoth of a building that had been a home for so long, and a taxi was there waiting for her. Asking him if he was able to take her someplace, he asked if she was PJ Brooks. After telling him that she was, he got out of the taxi.

"I'm to take you to your home, the one here in town that your father left for you." Nodding, she got in the back and waited for him to get the car started. "You're going to be met by two men when you get there. One is your attorney, and the other is your father's. I'm to tell you that there are clothes in the master bedroom for you, as well as anything else you might need to clean up."

"Why?" He asked her what she meant. "Any number of questions, I suppose. Why are they meeting me there? Why is there clothing for me? Why the master bedroom, and where might I be going that I have to clean up? Any or all questions you have an answer to would be nice."

"I don't know. I was just hired to pick you up today and give you the message they gave me." She nodded and looked out the window as he made his way down the road. "If you don't mind me saying so, you look pretty good for a woman that has spent the last ten years in prison."

Nodding, not even sure how she was supposed to respond to that, or even if she should, she thought about going home. She wanted to find someplace else to spend her first night out, anywhere but where Angela was. Parker thought about asking him where she was in all this, but didn't really care all that much.

He tossed back a box to her. "Cell phone. It's charged and programmed with a few numbers. And I'm to tell you that there are a few pictures you might want to take a look at before you get home. And I'm sorry, I don't know what they are of, nor who put them on there." She asked about her stepmother. "I didn't see anyone else but those two men when I was called there."

Parker pulled the phone out of the box and turned it on. It was something that she'd had before going in, but they'd changed so much that she was afraid of breaking it. Almost as soon as it was on, it rang. The name that came up was Joseph March, Da's attorney. She ignored it for the pictures.

They were of her and her da. Fishing trips that they'd taken. A few times a year he'd go out on the boat with her, too. She was nearly at the end of them when the phone rang again—this time it said Allen Blackwell. Not wanting to talk to him either, she let it go.

When they were pulling up in front of the mansion that was now hers, or so she'd been told, the two men came out to stand on the porch that surrounded the house. She didn't know what they wanted, but she wanted a shower in the worst kind of way, and a meal that didn't make a slop sound when put on her plate.

"Maggie still here?" Blackwell nodded and smiled at her. "Whatever is going on that brings you both out here? Can I get something to eat and a shower? Unless this is about Angela. If so, I'm not ready to talk about her."

"Angela has been put out." She looked at March and asked him what he'd said. "Put out. The will that your father made out the month before he died stated that she was to get nothing of the estate. Also that she was to be, and I quote, 'Put to the curb without anything that she didn't come to him with.'"

She went into the house and could smell her da's cigars. The cologne that he wore when he'd shave. Parker went into his study and inhaled deeply. Tears filled her eyes, and she thought of the only man that she'd ever love. Before she made too much more of a fool of herself, she went to see Maggie to ask her for something to eat.

The two of them hugged tightly, several times. She wasn't used to being touched so much, so it took her a moment not to flinch back from her. Maggie was crying, which brought Parker's tears to the surface, and she headed up to the master bedroom to take a shower and get cleaned up.

The room was devoid of anything but the bed and

furniture. There were no pictures on the walls, and the knickknacks that her da had were gone as well. His books were also gone from the shelves in the room.

After cleaning up, she dressed in clothing that she would have to get used to, things that fit her, and the shoes were soft tennis shoes, the kind that she had loved before all of this. Going down to the kitchen again, both men were there waiting.

"Can we talk while you eat?" Nodding to them both, she took a bite of the roast beef sandwich that had been made for her, and thought she'd gone to heaven. Blackwell spoke first. "The money has been transferred to your account. The houses, all six of them, have been transferred to your name as well. We have a meeting downtown at six to sign all the paperwork that establishes you as head of the corporation that your father built. The rest is right here; if you have any questions on that, let me know."

She picked up the sheath of papers and laid them back down. Parker would read them over, but not right this minute. Finishing up the sandwich, she leaned back in her chair.

"What's happened to my da's room? There is nothing in there to even show that he was living here. Even his books are missing." March cleared his throat and looked uncomfortable. "Look, I would have just as soon not come here at all. But knowing that Angela isn't here makes it better. Spill it."

"When the will was read for your father, Angela had assumed that she'd get a large share of the company and the homes. Before that, even before the funeral was set up, she had the room cleaned out and put together the way she wanted it. All the things in the room where sold or given away. I'm terribly sorry, PJ." Her heart broke for all Da's things. She asked them to call her Parker. "She'd had a team lined up to come and strip the entire house of you and your father. Then when the will was read, and she found out that she got nothing and wasn't going to be able to live here, she went a little crazy. Violently. She was arrested, and since she was let out, she's been causing all kinds of trouble, not only around here but at the company as well. Angela has since been barred from all the companies that you now own."

"Where is she now?" They didn't look like they were going to answer her. "Am I going to have to look over my shoulder for the rest of my life? Where is she?"

"She was able to purchase a house about a mile from here. We're still trying to figure out how she had the funds for that, but there is nothing missing from here or the company." Parker stretched her neck. "This is not the homecoming that your father wanted for you, child. Things have gone on here that frankly, I'm glad that you're back to take care of."

"The board of directors, they know that I've been in prison, no doubt. Do you suppose they'll want me out?" March shook his head with a huge smile. "Da told them that I was taking it for him, didn't he?"

"Yes, he did. They have been sworn to keep it to themselves. That's the only people that we think he told. Besides us. You can expect a warm welcome from them, I'm sure." He handed her a thick file, and she knew what it was immediately. "There is everything we could get on the trial and the sentencing hearing. There are so many things wrong with it that I'm surprised that you didn't take them to heel. You are a good attorney."

"Not any more. I'm an ex-con, remember?" Both men nodded and Parker stood up. "I'm going to go to bed for a while. This meeting, I'll go to it, but I would like you both there as well."

"Yes, all right. We'll be there." They both stood up and started to leave. March turned and looked at her with a smile. "I'm glad that you're home, Parker. Your father, he was so proud of you. And had such high hopes that someone would come forward with information."

Nodding, she headed up to bed. It would be nice to sleep uninterrupted for a few hours. Lying on the bed, she thought of Angela. If she thought that she was going to get by with anything with her, she was going to be in for a very rude awakening.

Before You Go...

HELP AN AUTHOR

write a review

THANK YOU!

Share your voice and help guide other readers to these wonderful books. Even if it's only a line or two your reviews help readers discover the author's books so they can continue creating stories that you'll love. Login to your favorite retailer and leave a review. Thank you.

AWARD WINNING, BESTSELLING AUTHOR

Kathi Barton, winner of the Pinnacle Book Achievement award as well as a best-selling author on Amazon and All Romance books, lives in Nashport, Ohio with her husband Paul. When not creating new worlds and romance, Kathi and her husband enjoy camping and going to auctions. She can also be seen at county fairs with her husband who is an artist and potter.

Her muse, a cross between Jimmy Stewart and Hugh Jackman, brings her stories to life for her readers in a way that has them coming back time and again for more. Her favorite genre is paranormal romance with a great deal of spice. You can visit Kathi online and drop her an email if you'd like. She loves hearing from her fans. aaronskiss@gmail.com.

Follow Kathi on her blog: http://kathisbartonauthor. blogspot.com/